Never Judge a Beast by His Cover

The Three Graces
Book 2

Alanna Lucas

DRAGONBLADE PUBLISHING, INC.

ARE YOU SIGNED UP FOR DRAGONBLADE'S BLOG?

You'll get the latest news and information on exclusive giveaways, exclusive excerpts, coming releases, sales, free books, cover reveals and more.

Check out our complete list of authors, too!

No spam, no junk. That's a promise!

Sign Up Here

www.dragonbladepublishing.com

Dearest Reader;

Thank you for your support of a small press. At Dragonblade Publishing, we strive to bring you the highest quality Historical Romance from some of the best authors in the business. Without your support, there is no 'us', so we sincerely hope you adore these stories and find some new favorite authors along the way.

Happy Reading!

CEO, Dragonblade Publishing

Additional Dragonblade books by Author Alanna Lucas

The Three Graces Series
A Most Improper Duchess (Book 1)
Never Judge a Beast by His Cover (Book 2)

The Lyon's Den Series
How to Steal a Lyon's Fortune

⁂

Chapter One

THEODORA GRACE HAD been looking forward to this evening's entertainments hosted by Lord Grimsby in honor of his nephew, Mr. Eastwick, ever since the invitation arrived at her aunt's home. It wasn't that she hadn't enjoyed the Season thus far—although, truth be told, she would rather be in the country at her beloved Charis with her sisters, but that time had passed and it was her sister-in-law's home now. No, it was because tonight was the night that she and her sisters, Alexandra and Evelina, would enact their plan to bring their dear friend, Naomi, and Mr. Norley together. The sisters were certain that the pair had formed a *tendre*, but since Naomi was the sister of a duke and Mr. Norley the second son of a baron, her mother, the Dowager Duchess of Blackburn, was certain to object to the match. The dowager even objected to the three Grace sisters, and they were the daughters of a viscount.

Theodora could hardly contain her restlessness, bouncing her foot as the carriage progressed at a snail's pace through the busy streets of London. When would they arrive? Her two sisters appeared just as fidgety as she, their feet tapping in the same rhythm as hers.

"Patience, dearies, patience," Aunt Imogene recited numerous times during the slow journey. "There still will be plenty of dancing once we arrive."

Theodora wasn't concerned about dancing—she had more important things to accomplish this evening. There would be time enough for such entertainments after the sisters had played matchmaker. She continued to tap her foot, hoping the distraction would ease the excited anticipation coursing through her veins. It felt as if they'd been trudging along for several hours.

She was about to ask how much farther when Aunt Imogene announced with gusto, "We've arrived!"

A not so short time later, the party of four was entering the grand—albeit rather somber-colored—ballroom to the lively sounds of a quadrille. They moved to a less occupied portion of the room and watched as the dance was coming to an end.

"It is quite the crush this evening," Evelina commented behind her blue and white lace-trimmed fan as she scanned the room before her eyes settled on an approaching gentleman. "There he is. Remember the plan," Evelina remarked under her breath.

Theodora eyed the approaching Mr. Norley with curiosity. They'd been introduced at Lady Kirkwood's dinner party several nights previous. He cut a fine figure then, just as he did this evening in his formal attire, although a color other than brown breeches and coat would surely suit his dark brown hair and brown eyes better. He looked far too . . . earthy.

Mr. Norley greeted them, then turned his attention to Theodora. "May I have the pleasure of the next dance, Miss Theodora?" he asked in a pleasant tone which she found quite amiable.

"I would be most pleased, Mr. Norley." This was the opportunity she'd been hoping for. They had only walked a few paces when she questioned, "Are you familiar with Lady Naomi?" In her estimation, it was better to get straight to the point than to hem and haw over the reason she was here this evening. Nothing was ever accomplished by a demure countenance.

"I am." He said the two words with an air of uncertainty and excitement, followed by a wide smile. This was most hopeful. As they took their places on the dance floor, he added, "I hope my request does not offend, but I was hoping you could aid me in . . ." He gulped hard, then started again. "Aid me in—"

Just then, the music began, disrupting their conversation. It was a pleasant tune but one that required participants to change partners, making conversation difficult. Nevertheless, it was still enjoyable as couples maneuvered through the lively steps with perfection.

Once Theodora rejoined her partner, she encouraged him to speak, hopeful for what she wanted to hear. "I will not be offended in the least, Mr. Norley, to hear your question. How are you in need of aid?"

With that, his features relaxed. He opened his mouth as if to speak when the steps required them to change partners once again. *Oh, this was all becoming so vexing*, she inwardly sighed. If only couples could speak with ease off the dance floor without worry of stirring rumors and gossip.

Thankfully, the next time they rejoined, Mr. Norley uttered his request with haste. "Please help me find a moment to speak with Lady Naomi this evening." Even with all the chatter around them, Theodora could sense his words were sincere. If she had any doubts, his bright, hopeful smile reinforced his sentiments.

"Of course," she offered.

She needed to think quickly. Soon the dance would be at an end and propriety dictated that she be returned to her chaperone. Not that Aunt Imogene would mind her conversing with the gentleman, but the gossips' tongues would be wagging and that was something she wished to avoid. For as long as she lived, Theodora would never understand society's strict rules. How could she give the couple a moment to talk, to—

That's it!

As the music softened and came to an end, Mr. Norley walked her back to where her relatives were. "Meet me in the refreshment hall in half an hour," she murmured for his ears only, careful not to alert any eavesdroppers, or worse, the Dowager Duchess of Blackburn.

Mr. Norley nodded his head in understanding, then took his leave with a light step.

With her plan in motion, Theodora was able to relax and take in the festivities. The joyful laughter and happy faces were in direct contrast to the room with its dark mahogany walls and ceiling. She found it odd that there were no mirrors hanging to reflect the candlelight. Her gaze swept across the room, settling on a darkish corner. Could Lord Grimsby not afford enough candles? Surely that could not be—

A movement, ever so slight as it was, caught her attention. She narrowed her gaze, focusing in that direction, and spied a rather large figure shrouded in darkness. Half his face appeared covered. *Was he wearing a mask?*

"Who is that?" Theodora questioned as she elbowed Alexandra, trying to acquire her eldest sister's attention. "Over there, in the shadows?"

"That is Lord Grimsby, *the* Earl of Grimsby. He hasn't been seen in Society in years." Aunt Imogene then tsked several times, her words weighed down in grief. "Such a tragic story."

Theodora pulled her gaze from the earl's corner and glanced at their great-aunt. "What happened?"

Aunt Imogene leaned in and told the unfortunate tale. "Nearly twelve years ago, there was a terrible fire at the hunting lodge on the Grimsby Hall estate. Lord Grimsby rescued his mother and younger sister and a servant from the blaze, but when he tried to rescue his brother and father, he was injured by debris. He pulled them out of the house, but neither survived. That is why he wears a mask, keeps to the shadows, and avoids society. Some call him the Phantom of Grimsby Hall, while others call him a beast because of his height and supposed temper."

Pain and sorrow struck her heart with Aunt Imogene's words. Theodora continued to watch the dark corner. What had he endured through the years? What had become of his mother and sister? Had he isolated himself from everyone or had his disfigurement caused everyone to turn from him? And after all this time, what was he doing in London? She wondered what sort of man rushed into a burning home, to save those he loved, but then avoided human contact. So many thoughts and questions swirled through her mind.

"What is he doing in London, *and* hosting a ball if he wants to avoid society?" Alexandra asked one of the many questions that was on Theodora's mind. She studied the dark corner of the room where the lone figure watched those enjoying his hospitality. What must he be thinking? How truly desolate it must be to stand alone, concealed in gloom, as merriment surrounds you, mocks you.

Aunt Imogene began to explain, "To find a suitable match for his cousin and heir, Mr. Eastwick. Lady Archibald told me that he has vowed to never marry, but wants to ensure the earldom is secure. He is very dedicated to his family's legacy and the running of their numerous estates." Their aunt shifted her gaze between her and Alexandra. "Perhaps one of you would suit Mr. Eastwick. He is quite handsome, and with what he stands to inherit—"

Theodora's gaze snapped to her aunt's. "I have no intention on marrying just because a gentleman is handsome or wealthy. What matters most is what's on the inside, in his heart. Is he a good man? A caring man?" She didn't want to marry because someone was pleasant looking. She wanted to marry because of shared interests, for desire and love.

Their discussion was interrupted by the return of Evelina and Mr. Greenford, who had been dancing. By his rigid and annoyed features, Theodora presumed the dance did not go at all well for Mr. Greenford. A moment later, her suspicions were confirmed when said gentleman offered a stiff bow, then stormed off.

A single brow raised in question as Alexandra spoke, "What happened on the dance floor?"

"Mr. Greenford was far too interested in boasting about the size of his estate and how much he spent on renovations, rather than in a simple conversation about poetry." Evelina huffed with annoyance.

Theodora would have enjoyed hearing more of her sister's account of the dance and conversation, but she spied Naomi without her domineering mother and needed to speak to her about Mr. Norley's request. She was not going to let this opportunity pass her friend by. Theodora was certain Evelina would recount the experience later when the sisters returned to the quiet of their rooms.

Unfortunately, by the time Theodora edged through the crush and neared Naomi, her mother had returned from her conversation with Lady Gordon, and was now standing sentinel at her side. Fortunately, the dowager had yet to notice Theodora, but how would she be able to talk to her friend without her formidable mother overhearing?

Theodora thought for a moment and settled on nonchalance. A casual stroll about the ballroom with an accidental bump into Naomi should allow for some conversation. She sucked in a deep breath and hoped this would work.

As she enacted her plan and strolled toward Naomi, she was acutely aware of the dark corner. Who was Lord Grimsby watching? What was he thinking? How did he endure events such as these? Did he always keep to the shadows or was it only at social functions? What joy did he have in his life?

So caught up in her own thoughts, she hadn't been paying attention to where she was walking and bumped right into—

"Miss Theodora, what a pleasant surprise," Naomi greeted with enthusiasm, and a hint of relief. Clearly her friend was in need of escaping her mother's domineering grasp.

Theodora's plan was working better than she had planned. Before she could respond, her friend took her arm and guided her a couple of feet away from the dowager. It wasn't far enough in her estimation, but it should afford them a little privacy.

"I was hoping to speak with you. I saw you dancing with"— Naomi's low whisper then lowered even further—"Mr. Norley."

Out of the corner of her eye, she spied the dowager watching their interaction with concerned interest. How in the world did her friend endure a parent such as her? And then she started moving toward them, a scowl dominating her features. There was no time to lose.

"Meet him in the refreshment hall in quarter of an hour," Theodora uttered with haste, the last word exiting her mouth just as Naomi's mother reached them. "Good evening, Your Grace. You look quite lovely in that shade of nacarat." She offered the pleasantry in the sweetest tone she could muster, given who Theodora was speaking to.

The older woman did not say a word, but eyed them both for several long seconds as if assessing their true intent. "I require your attention over here, Naomi." And then she walked away, expecting her daughter to follow without protest.

Naomi mouthed an apology, then went to her mother's side. Theodora had her doubts, but hopefully Naomi would be able to meet Mr. Norley. Theodora would stay close at hand just in case she was needed to distract the dowager. How she would achieve that monumental task, she didn't quite know, but she would think of something.

Just then Aunt Imogene rushed to her side with a very handsome young gentleman in tow. "Mr. Eastwick, allow me to introduce my great-niece, Miss Theodora Grace."

Oh dear, was Aunt Imogene actually serious about a match between her and Mr. Eastwick? And just after Theodora had stated so plainly that she would not be swayed by a handsome face.

"The pleasure is all mine," Mr. Eastwick said with a nervous quaver. "May . . . may I have the pleasure of the next dance, Miss Theodora?"

Her relative's bright, encouraging smile laced with guilt—undoubtedly for practically dragging poor Mr. Eastwick across the room—said it all. But Theodora would not punish the gentleman because of her aunt's subterfuge.

"I would be delighted," she said as she took the offered arm. As they strolled toward the dance floor, she caught the gleam of hope in her relative's eye. Aunt Imogene was quite incorrigible at times.

Before long, they were dancing through the ballroom amongst hushed whispers, and all because she was dancing with the guest of honor. Theodora truly did not understand the ways of the *ton* at times.

As they rounded one corner, she thought she heard Mrs. Fleming comment, rather loudly, about what a lovely couple she and Mr. Eastwick made. Oh dear, she must be careful. Not that she minded Mr. Eastwick. He *was* handsome and seemed pleasant, but she felt no spark, nothing like her mother described in her love letters to father. Of course, they only had just met. These things may take time, but something deep within told her otherwise. Perhaps this was a topic to discuss at their secret salon.

Once again, her musings had distracted her from the present. However, Mr. Eastwick did not seem to mind as the silence lingered on through the dance. The nervous worry lines beside his eyes and constant bobbing of his Adam's apple suggested he was not comfortable at social gatherings. He was a lovely dancer, though.

When the dance came to an end, he swallowed hard, offered a pleasantry, then dashed off to the dark corner, presumably to converse with his cousin. What a peculiar young man Mr. Eastwick was.

Loud sobs ricocheted from behind. She turned to see who the source was when she caught sight of the Dowager Duchess of Blackburn pulling her daughter away from a stunned Mr. Norley who was left holding two glasses of lemonade.

Worse still was the dowager's loud proclamation that no daughter of duke would ever associate with such riffraff as an untitled gentleman as it reverberated through the ballroom. What started as a pleasant evening full of hope for her friend was quickly souring. Could this evening get any worse?

THIS EVENING IS a necessary torture, Damian kept reminding himself from his dark corner of the ballroom. He could endure one Season of gossip to ensure the earldom would survive. Although his young cousin was . . . well, young and inexperienced, even at the tender age of nineteen, Horatio possessed strong morals. Damian's successor would serve the title and the responsibilities that came with it well. Part of him wanted to wait until Horatio was older, more mature, to introduce him into Society, but the past had taught Damian that one could never be certain what the future held. He just needed to encourage the painfully shy lad.

He watched Horatio throughout the evening, making mental notes on how he could improve his countenance and confidence. He was certain after attending a couple of events, Horatio would feel more at ease in this world. Damian had been grooming his elder cousin for the role of earl for several years, but Victor's untimely death made it necessary for Horatio to now take on that responsibility. Not that Damian was in his dotage, but one could never be certain what the good Lord had in store for them.

In a previous life, one not dictated by a mask, Damian had enjoyed Town. Not the balls, but the opera and musicales. Before his elder brother died, Damian had had dreams of becoming a great composer. But in one fiery afternoon, both his father and brother had been snatched from his family, and his constant nightmare had begun. Restless nights, hurt and betrayal, regret that he could not save them—desperation and despair had been consuming every breath he took for years.

Be strong. Remember why you are here.

Damian shoved those thoughts to the murky recess of his mind. There would be time enough to relive the past, for it never left him, not even for a day.

Turning his attention to the present, he watched with interest as Horatio and a very attractive lady danced in perfect harmony through the ballroom. They were well-paired for the dance. He'd noticed her earlier when her gaze had centered on his dark corner. Who was she?

Not that he expected his cousin to find a suitable countess after one event, but it was promising that Horatio was actually dancing—his first of the evening—and not cowering in the corner waiting until the evening came to a close. Damian didn't know how to help the lad overcome his shyness. Perhaps all he needed was to catch the eye of a young lady.

Although there was always room for improvement, this evening was not the disaster Damian first envisioned. It gave him hope for the rest of the Season.

It wasn't even as if Damian was expecting his cousin to make an announcement by the end of the Season. He would not be unreasonable. They had, however, come to an agreement that if by the end, Horatio was not prepared to choose a bride, he would present a list of suitable ladies that would then be invited to a country house party.

The heavy weight of responsibility to ensure the earldom pressed against his chest, stifling his breathing. He could endure playing host for a short duration. He must.

Damian would not think about all the details at present.

As the music began, he closed his eyes, feeling it invade his innermost being. Many would deem tonight's octet as a necessary means to dance, but for Damian, music was ambrosia for the soul. He inhaled deeply, as each note and chord coursed through him, soothing him. Soon the sound became a full orchestra, flooding his senses.

So lost in the moment, he hadn't realized the dance had come to an end until his cousin was at his side. "I did my duty and danced, may I please retire?" Horatio pleaded, sounding more like a child of five than a man of nineteen.

"It would not be appropriate for the host to retire while guests are still present." He sensed an argument forthcoming, but before it began, he raised a hand to stop his cousin. "You will never feel comfortable at these events unless you try."

It really was unfair of him to demand so much from someone so young and unaccustomed to this world. Horatio loved being on the sea, feeling the ocean mist caress his face and the gentle rolling waves calm his body. It was quite a poetic sentiment and one Horatio had mentioned at a dozen times since arriving in London. Damian gazed across the guests. This sea of colorful plumes lapping through the crush offered no such serenity.

"For you, I will try." And with that sullen remark, he trudged from their dark corner back into the gaiety of society.

As the evening progressed, Damian knew he could not stay sequestered in his unlit niche, and so, regardless of the mask he wore, he reluctantly edged away from his alcove of obscurity and greeted his guests.

It went as expected with the ladies nervously glancing away, almost in fear of the half-mask he wore. That is, until he was introduced to Lady Middleton and her nieces. The conversation started as all the others, thank you for the invitation, your home is lovely, your cousin is amiable. It was as if they all had memorized the same lines from a play. But when Miss Theodora spoke, something changed.

"The entertainment for tonight is quite exquisite. I particularly enjoyed *The Nameless*. That particular tune has a sense of lightheartedness that I found quite appealing."

Damian had not thought of the dance in that light, but he was intrigued by Miss Theodora's explanation. "You enjoy music?" Of course, she did. Every debutante did. It was expected of them to dance as well, displaying their talents in the marriage mart game.

"I believe it a requirement, Lord Grimsby," she teased, mirroring his thoughts, and then her tone turned, almost sensual. "But in all seriousness, yes, music feeds my soul."

Those last words brushed past her lips and settled into his being. His heart gave a fierce thud, demanding attention as his gaze met Miss Theodora's passionate blue eyes. She was a dangerous distraction. And one he could not afford. His dreams had been shattered and broken once before. The path he was on now was one he walked alone.

"It was a pleasure meeting you, ladies. Enjoy the rest of the evening." And with that, Damian walked away, adding another layer to the wall around his heart.

━━━━━❦━━━━━

Chapter Two

MONTHS, AND FAR too many balls, soirées, and dinners later, the Season was finally at an end. As Damian had suspected, Horatio did begin—albeit only slightly—to feel more at ease amongst the *ton*. However, he had not set his cap on any one Miss in particular and so presented his list of ladies—ones he believed were sincere in their attention. Not wasting any time, invites to the country house party Damian was to host were sent a couple of weeks before they were to depart London.

Damian wasn't surprised at the enthusiastic responses. Word had quickly circulated just how wealthy Damian was and how prosperous the earldom was—and that he was searching for a bride for his cousin. Much to both his and Horatio's displeasure, the latter had become quite popular, and not in the way they'd hoped. Fortune hunters and title climbers had practically pounded down their door for the remainder of the Season.

Horatio had frequently reminded Damian that he would not take offense if Damian decided to marry and sire many heirs. Damian knew without a doubt his young cousin would have preferred to live a quiet existence, preferably at sea. He hoped that with time and experience—and patience—the lad would learn how to manage the earldom and grow to love the land as much as he.

"Come on, Shadow," Damian called to his dog as he exited his London house. "It's time to return home." The dog's tail went wild with the mention of home. Perhaps he'd been selfish in bringing his rather large dog to Town, but he had not wanted to be parted from his constant companion for an entire Season.

"I do not know who's more excited to leave—you, me, or the dog," Horatio said with a chuckle as he joined Damian and Shadow in the large, crested carriage. Before long, they were leaving London behind in pursuit of the peaceful countryside.

"Town certainly does not hold the luster of years past," Damian admitted, the melancholy edging into his words. His life had changed quite drastically since the last time he'd journeyed to London. He used to be able to move about without worry of comments about the fire, his mother's suffering, or how he used to look. He didn't want to think about the past. He needed to concentrate on the present and aiding his cousin in making a match was the only task at hand. "Have you given any more thought about which lady—"

"Would make a suitable countess?"

"Has caught your eye," Damian corrected with firmness. "Suitability is of course a factor, but above all else, I want you to marry for love. Duties can be learned, love is precious."

Years ago, his mother had told him that he was a romantic at heart. Perhaps he was, but that was how he believed all matches should be made. His parents had married for love, and so had his sister. He'd thought he'd found love once, as well, but it turned out to be fleeting. Justine had abandoned him in his darkest hour, crying that he looked more beast than man.

His cousin was silent for long seconds, his features crinkled in deep contemplation, before answering. "Miss Ashton and Miss O'Donnell are both amiable. Miss Raine is very agreeable. And of course, there is Miss Grace." He paused for a moment, then clarified. "The youngest Miss Grace, Miss Theodora Grace."

Ah yes, Miss Theodora Grace.

At every event they'd both attended, she'd tried to engage

Damian in conversation with talk of music and melodies. And at every event, he'd managed to shield himself, and hie away before thoughts of her intelligence, beauty, and sweet smile affected him. There was something about her he couldn't resist. Every time she looked his way, it was as if she were trying to see inside his soul, and he lost himself in those caring deep blue eyes.

He stamped down feelings he hadn't felt in years and cleared his throat. "All good choices. We should discuss how we are to proceed at the house party. Aunt Esther arrived last week and has been setting the house to rights. Invitations will be going out for the grand ball to the families in the county and—"

"This all seems so tedious." His cousin let out a long huff. "There must be a better, more practical way to go about all this."

"You won't feel that way once the festivities begin," Damian tried to convince his cousin, as well as himself. "You needn't worry. Aunt Esther is handling everything."

Another long huff filled the carriage as Horatio crossed his arms and slid into the corner and closed his eyes, clearly not wanting to discuss the upcoming festivities further.

Without a doubt, Damian could tell that Horatio was still not entirely comfortable in this new world of the *ton*. Damian could not blame the lad. Horatio had not been born and groomed to be an earl, or even a spare, but this was his lot now. But he knew that with their widowed aunt's assistance, the country party would be a great success.

THE CLOUDLESS SUMMER day was most glorious as they traveled along toward their destination at a gentle pace. Their first London Season was behind them, along with all the constant social obligations and seemingly never-ending gossip.

Theodora took in a deep, relaxing breath as she watched the passing countryside. Oh, how she missed the fresh country air and peacefulness of nature. Finally feeling more like herself, she was able to reflect on all that had happened over the past months.

"What do you think Alexandra is doing right now?" The words slipped from Theodora's mouth without thought.

"Enjoying married life and learning her new role as the Duchess of Blackburn," Aunt Imogene said as she shifted toward the sisters. "The Blackburn estate is quite large. She has many new duties now. You will see her soon enough at Christmas."

"I do miss her, though," Theodora said. The sisters had never before been apart, not even for a night. Still, she was quite happy for her eldest sister. Alexandra and Niall were the best of friends, and she knew they would have a beautiful life together.

"I do, too," Evelina agreed, a tinge of sadness lingered on her words.

"Listen to you girls," Aunt Imogene playfully scolded. "You sound rather melancholy considering we're traveling to a house party." She smiled widely and clasped her hands together as she eyed Evelina for a moment before settling her gaze on Theodora. "I'm pleased to see you've changed your mind about Mr. Eastwick."

Evelina shook her head slightly, having already voiced her opinion that Mr. Eastwick would not suit her, especially considering he was three years her junior, but thankfully did not say a word. She was far too argumentative lately whenever the opposite sex, making a match, or marriage was mentioned. Worse still, Evelina was reluctant to share her thoughts with anyone. Theodora, on the other hand, was not reluctant or argumentative, she just knew her mind and would not settle.

Although Great-aunt Imogene, who had only been briefly married to Lord Middleton before his untimely death, did not care for being married herself, she wanted her great-nieces each to have a happy union like their parents. And she was most insistent that the sisters discovered love in her lifetime.

"I am certain Mr. Eastwick will make a fine husband." She spoke as if Theodora and Mr. Eastwick had an understanding—

which they certainly did not.

Theodora offered a simple nod and smile in return. She wasn't about to tell her relative that she hadn't changed her mind with regard to a possible union with Mr. Eastwick. He was a pleasant fellow, and she did not see a reason not to accept the invitation to Grimsby Hall. Many of her friends had been invited, and Theodora and Evelina decided that attending the house party would allow them to aid their friends in finding matches. Plus, she was curious about Lord Grimsby.

Ever since she'd first spied him, she wanted to know him— not the rumors, but the man. Aunt Imogene had said he was a great lover of music, and although they'd had only a brief conversation at his London home, she wanted to discuss music with him. It was one thing to enjoy music and quite another to appreciate the essence of the sounds created by the notes played. She'd met very few people who enjoyed composing and playing music as much as she. However, at every event during the Season that they'd both attended, he would say very little then disappear. At least he wouldn't be able to avoid her at his home. Well, she hoped not.

Several hours in companionable silence passed before the carriage turned down a long drive. Theodora peered out the carriage window and spied Grimsby Hall, standing impressively large in the distance. The exterior façade was a combination of cream and buff-colored bricks, with a hint of blue-green on some of the stones. There was something soothing about the color combination and Theodora wondered if the pattern and color choice were planned or happy chance.

The long drive gave Theodora the opportunity to take in the surrounding grounds. There were several tree-lined avenues that veered off the main drive. She wondered where they led to and what adventures were to be had there.

As they approached their destination, she shifted her focus to the house, studying its massive four-story façade. Its impressive u-shaped design with its many windows would allow plenty of natural light to invade the space.

In many regards, it was the exact opposite of what she'd expected given how formal and dark Lord Grimsby's home in London was. Would he continue to keep to the shadows, avoiding guests? Or would he engage in activities and be social? Theodora suspected it would be the former, especially after Aunt Imogene told her the story of the great tragedy and his lengthy recovery. She'd since learned that once Lord Grimsby was strong enough, he'd had what was left of the hunting lodge torn down. All that remained were mere ruins.

Theodora could not escape the thoughts of what he must have endured, how much he'd suffered. At the various events they'd attended during the Season, she had tried to talk to him, but he'd always avoided her. But she didn't want to pry, she wanted to offer understanding. She saw the pain in his eyes and knew that pain in her heart. She'd felt it every day her father had suffered through his illness. She hoped being at Grimsby Hall would allow for some conversation, perhaps friendship even. In her estimation, one could never have too many true friends.

"By the looks of it, several guests have already arrived." Aunt Imogene's excited words echoed through the conveyance. She then pressed her nose to the glass like a small child, trying to get a better look at those who had arrived. "Oh, there's Lady Vernon and her daughter, Lady Danielle. I do enjoy their company. I believe you will find Lady Danielle most agreeable. Such a sweet girl."

No sooner had the ladies alighted from their carriages, than a friendly-looking older woman, dressed in a deep shade of aubergine, greeted them at the top of the steps. "Welcome ladies, I am Lady Stanbourne, Lord Grimsby and Mr. Eastwick's aunt. Your rooms have been readied. After a brief rest, I will give you a tour of the house, after which my nephews will join us. They are currently handling some estate business."

Once settled in their rooms, Aunt Imogene decided upon a nap, while Theodora and Evelina took the opportunity to discuss the guests who'd already arrived. Although quite a few were good friends who had even been invited to attend their secret salons in London, others were mere acquaintances.

"Even though we most likely won't have the opportunity to host our salon here, we should not refrain from aiding our friends if the opportunity presents itself. However, we should err on the side of caution with those we are not familiar with," Evelina suggested.

With that agreed upon, they began to ready themselves for evening. Although neither sister was in need of new clothes for the country house party, Aunt Imogene had thought it would be best if the sisters each had several new dresses for the occasion. Tonight, Theodora was to wear a lovely celestial blue British net dress over the same blue sarsnet slip. She simply adored the way the colors subtly changed as she moved and had been looking forward to wearing the creation ever since it had arrived from the modiste some weeks past.

A short time later, Theodora, Evelina, and Aunt Imogene were much refreshed and had joined several other of the guests for a tour of Grimsby Hall. Lady Stanbourne was an excellent and informative hostess, pointing out various artworks, statues, and paintings, while giving a history of the house and architectural elements.

They came to a stop in front of a portrait of a beautiful young woman with eyes like the sea on calm day. Her slight, upturned smile suggested a hint of mischievousness, while her posture and architectural drawing on the table beside her declared that she was in charge of the vast estate that was depicted in the background.

"Who is this?" Lady Danielle questioned in a reserved tone.

"That is Marina de Harcourt, the first Countess of Grimsby. The first Earl of Grimsby had this home built for his bride, or rather, gave her *carte blanche* to create a masterpiece to her liking," Lady Stanbourne started to explain. "It was said that Lady Grimsby wanted a home to rival Hardwick Hall. Hence the abundance of windows. No expense was spared."

"Was it a love match?" Lady O'Donnell asked as she eyed the portrait of the first Lady Grimsby.

"It is believed so," Lady Stanbourne said. "The Earls of Grimsby have been most blessed in marriage." There was a tinge of sadness in her words and, knowing the story of the current earl, Theodora could not help but wonder if his aunt hoped for more for her nephew.

As the tour continued, Theodora lost herself in the beauty of art that was in such abundance. Hundreds of years of accumulating these treasures had resulted in a magnificent collection.

All too soon, the tour came to an end and they reached the drawing room, where the others—who had not wanted to tour the house—had gathered.

Tea and refreshments were served while they waited for Lord Grimsby and Mr. Eastwick to arrive. Conversation and chatter from the dozens of guests filled the room. Unfortunately, it was much the same as in London. Talk of the weather and state of the roads were the order of the day. Theodora tried to insert comments about the artwork they'd just seen, but those present dismissed that topic, clearly not interested in discussing anything more stimulating.

Evelina leaned in toward Theodora and whispered, "I hope not all conversations will be this tedious, otherwise it will be an exasperating couple of weeks."

She wholeheartedly agreed, but before Theodora had a chance to respond, Mr. Eastwick entered the room.

"I apologize for my lateness," Mr. Eastwick said with nervousness as he halted just inside the drawing room. His aunt went to his side, which seemed to give him some confidence. "Thank you for joining us. I hope you will be most comfortable here."

Theodora noticed the normally shy and unsure gentleman appeared a little more at ease here in the country—not much, but some. She also could not help but notice that Lord Grimsby had not arrived with his cousin. She wondered if he would be keeping his distance, just as he had on previous occasions. She wanted to ask if he would be joining them but didn't want to appear rude. Thankfully, Lady Stanbourne answered her unspoken question.

"Lord Grimsby is still detained and will be joining us after dinner this evening and—"

Woof . . . woof . . .

Just then, a large charcoal-colored dog pranced into the room, tail wagging in excitement. Several ladies let out loud screams, which only excited the animal further. One would have thought they'd never seen a dog before.

The dog playfully jumped from guest to guest but as he neared Theodora, she held out her hand to allow him to sniff her.

"My sister has a way with animals," Evelina announced, trying to help calm the ladies in attendance.

Theodora allowed him to take his time, and before too long—realizing she was not a threat but was very much willing to pet him—the large dog sat next to her, enjoying the affection she was showering upon the harmless creature.

"You're quite handsome," she said as stroked the dog. "You didn't mean any harm, now did you?" she cooed, ignoring the hysterics still being spewed by some of the women.

"Perhaps there is someone to take that . . . that beast outside," Lady O'Donnell said in a quivering tone, while clutching her chest. Clearly, she was not fond of dogs.

Lady Stanbourne bent slightly and patted her side as she said, "Come on. That's enough excitement for the moment." The dog went to her side, his tail down. The dog obviously did not share the sentiment. She then turned to those present. "Dinner will be announced shortly. Please excuse me while I handle this . . . distraction." The last word exited her mouth in a giggle.

Only a short time later, Lady Stanbourne returned, so the only person missing was Lord Grimsby. Theodora had a feeling the elusive lord was not going to make an appearance this evening, but perhaps he would prove her wrong. Dinner was not to be announced for another fifteen minutes, so only a short time would tell.

Theodora and Evelina had never been to a country house party and didn't know quite what to expect. Aunt Imogene had shared that it was quite costly to entertain such a large group and for so long. It was clear that Lord Grimsby certainly had high hopes for securing a bride for his cousin. Dozens of people were already in attendance, and even more were expected to arrive on the morrow, including numerous gentlemen to round out the numbers. And then there were those who lived nearby but were not staying at Grimsby Hall. All in all, it was quite a large party.

Theodora was pleased that several of the ladies in attendance were already close acquaintances of her and Evelina's. They may not be able to host their regular salon while guests, but at the very least, the friends could carry on salon-worthy discussions, though not in the presence of their mamas of course. After some of the gossip that had circulated about Town this past Season, Theodora and Evelina had decided on a more clandestine approach in their quest for answers.

While Aunt Imogene became reacquainted with Lady Vernon, Theodora and Evelina occupied a spot near the window that overlooked one of the impressive gardens. It was an ideal location from which to view those present.

"Hopefully none of the gossips from Town were invited," Evelina said under her breath even as she pasted on a pleasant smile.

"I hope so, too. But given what we know about the earl, I don't believe he would tolerate such rumormongering in his home and—" Her thought was interrupted by the arrival of Miss Ashton.

"Miss Theodora, Miss Grace!" Miss Ashton rushed to where they were standing. "It's so nice to see you again—and so soon." She then lowered her voice and chattered on, "I do hope we will be able to continue our discussions. Oh, and include Lady Danielle and Miss O'Donnell. They find themselves in a similar circumstance as us. I'm eager to hear what Alexandra has shared."

That *similar circumstance* of course was the lack of knowledge young women were made privy to about men and the marriage bed. Despite the success of their salon, there were still many such details to uncover. And . . . much to the annoyance of Theodora and Evelina, their own sister had not shared any enlightening details after Alexandra married Niall. Remembrances of their pleading flashed through her thoughts.

"Why won't you share any of the details of your wedding night?" Theodora had implored her eldest sister.

But before Alexandra had had the opportunity to respond, Evelina continued the deluge of questioning. "Yes, why won't you give more details? How are we to understand the mysteries of men and marriage without your guidance? What exactly happens behind closed doors?"

And with that last question, Alexandra's cheeks had ripened into a deep blush. When her words had finally come, her voice was soft. "Oh dear, this is more difficult to talk about than I had thought." She paused for a moment then quickly added, "But not in a bad way. It is an . . . adjustment, and . . . very intimately private." Their eldest sister's tone then shifted to reassurance, the conviction in her words strong. It was a tone Theodora was familiar with, though it still wasn't helpful. "But I can share this, what we discovered at our salons is the truth. If you stay true to your heart's desire and marry for love, and welcome the passion that comes in the marriage bed, all will be well."

Why did it all have to be so cryptic?

Nonetheless, Theodora trusted her sister and hoped Alexandra was right. Now all she had to do was discover her heart's desire. But how would she know when she did?

"Miss Theodora? Is anything the matter?" Miss Ashton's question brought her back to the present.

Thankfully, Theodora didn't have to come up with a response because dinner was announced just then.

Everyone lined up and strolled toward the dining room. They'd learned earlier it was to be more casual this evening, with the meal being laid out in the small dining room. Upon entering the room, Theodora could not help but wonder what the large dining room looked like since this one boasted a table that could seat more than two dozen.

Although the balance of ladies to men was not equal, Theodora didn't mind, and she was certain her sister did not either. She was seated near Miss Ashton, while Evelina was seated near Miss Raine. It made for a very pleasant evening, even though Lord Grimsby was noticeably absent. The more he stayed away, the more curious Theodora was about the elusive earl.

Dinner passed with pleasant conversation, and afterward the men took brandy, while the ladies retreated to the drawing room. As Theodora entered the room, she noticed that one corner was not lit, though Lord Grimsby was not there. Would he be joining later? Would he keep to the shadows as he'd always had done while in London? These and other questions swirled through her mind.

Soon, the small group of men rejoined the ladies. Theodora was sitting in between Miss Ashton and Evelina, all the while eyeing the piano at the opposite end of the room. It had been nearly a week since she had last sat at an instrument and her fingers ached to play once again.

The conversation mostly centered on the ideal weather and the plans Lady Stanbourne had made for the duration of the party. They'd also been informed that Lord and Lady Hamilton were soon hosting a ball and all were invited, much to the delight of most of the young ladies present.

"I've heard Lord Hamilton is quite wealthy and his wife hosts the most extravagant balls," Miss Ashton leaned in and informed Theodora. "The invitations are most coveted. It is certain to be the highlight of the summer, and . . ."

The pleasant chatter that had been filling the room died to a soft hush as Lord Grimsby entered the room. All eyes focused on the masked earl. He was tall, taller than any of the men present, and quite Corinthian in stature. But what Theodora noticed was not his height, or even the mask he wore that covered the right side of his face, but the sadness in the depths of his clear blue eyes.

Lord Grimsby seemed frozen in place, unsure of whether he should proceed farther into the room, until Lady Stanbourne went to her nephew's side, and whispered something. His gaze scanned the room, meeting Theodora's for a breath of a moment. But in that moment, some upspoken communication passed between them before he schooled his features once again. Her heart pounded against her chest, demanding attention. She wondered if he felt the intensity of the connection, too.

He did not take another step into the room as he cleared his voice and said, "Thank you for accepting our invitation. I hope you enjoy your time at Grimsby Hall." And with that, Lord Grimsby turned and took his leave.

A pang of sympathy struck Theodora's heart as hushed murmurs rose about his scarred features. Lady Stanbourne and Mr. Eastwick quickly tried to divert the conversation with the enticement of card games. But what whispers and rumors had Lord Grimsby endured over the years, when his relatives could not come to his aid?

$$\text{Chapter Three}$$

THE SILENCE OF night filled the house. Although Theodora desperately wanted rest, sleep continued to evade her. When at home, she would wander the house and garden, but this wasn't her home—and it was still the middle of the night—so she settled on pacing the length of the hall outside her room. She could not stop thinking about Lord Grimsby and the way the guests had stared at him in silence, then spoke in hushed tones about his appearance once he'd gone.

Theodora did not keep track of how much time had passed or how many turns about the hall she'd taken, but when her feet began to ache, she went back to her room and attempted to go back to bed.

After lying in bed, eyes wide open, for several hours, Theodora decided sleep would never come. As the sun rose, she decided she'd refrained long enough. An early morning stroll was just what she needed. She stretched her limbs and went to the window. The sun had just crept above the eastern horizon, bathing the landscape in early morning hues. Billowy clouds caressed the dawning sky.

It promised to be a glorious day.

She opened the window, allowing the day to infiltrate her room and refresh her mind. The sounds of early morning were always calming. The world had not quite begun its day, and everything seemed to move at a slower pace.

Woof . . . woof . . .

She heard the dog before she spied the creature prancing across the lawn in the distance, with Lord Grimsby following close behind.

She watched as he chased and played with the dog. Even from this distance, he cut a fine figure. She'd noticed his height before, yet despite his size, there was a gentleness about him that she found most alluring. She was enjoying watching this interaction between man and beast. They seemed to enjoy one another's company.

She'd already made up her mind before she'd spied the pair that a morning walk would do her good, and she would not let their presence deter her. She would give them their privacy and simply go in the opposite direction. After donning one of her serviceable dresses that she could put on without the aid of a lady's maid, she put on her walking boots, then grabbed her father's coat. She knew her sister would not be surprised to find Theodora had left, so she scribbled a note for Evelina before slipping out her door.

It didn't take long to sneak out of the house—carefully avoiding servants who were preparing for the day—and into the crisp early morning. She inhaled the scents of the countryside, instantly feeling rejuvenated. Her thoughts became clearer, not so weighed down by the emotions that had kept her awake during the night.

Theodora started down a gravel path leading in the opposite direction of where she'd seen Lord Grimsby. The path narrowed slightly and then she came to a fork in the road. Staying straight would take her on a path with sporadic trees dotting the landscape that looked far too ordinary, so she opted for the tree lined walking path that quickly swept wide to the left, hiding what lay in the distance.

She walked in silence, enjoying the calm morning when all of sudden a loud *woof* echoed from beyond. No sooner had the sound reached her ears than the rather large charcoal dog dashed out of the bushes.

"Well, hello there." The dog came up to her, tail wagging fervently, clearly wanting affection. "Oh, so you remember me from yesterday," she said as she kneeled down beside the large animal and began to pet him.

She had purposely ventured in the opposite direction from man and dog, not wanting to intrude on Lord Grimsby's morning, but she couldn't help but wonder if he was nearby? Several pleasant minutes in the company of the dog passed before she discovered the answer to her question.

"What are you doing roaming outside at this early hour?" His voice rumbled through the calm countryside. Although his words were tinged with anger, his soulful eyes told a different story. A story of a man in need of friendship, understanding, compassion.

"I couldn't sleep," she said as she stood and continued to pet the dog.

"There are plenty of places inside the house to pass the hours. One of the libraries, or music room, or any number of places where you would be safe."

Theodora argued. "I'm safe out here. My sister knows where I went and—"

"You've been wandering alone?" He glanced around as if only just noticing that Theodora was indeed by herself.

"Not entirely." She leaned down and stroked the dog's head. "I've had some company." She looked over to where Lord Grimsby stood. He wore the same style of leather half-mask he'd worn on other occasions, only in a different shade. She was curious about the design. It was quite unique and beautifully fabricated, but she didn't want to offend. She wanted to gain his friendship. "What's his name?" she asked as she rubbed the dog's face between her hands. "You must have a name, don't you?" she cooed in a sweet voice that the dog seemed to enjoy.

AN EARLY MORNING walk had always been part of Damian's morning ritual, but had become an absolute necessity since the arrival of so many guests, and it had only been a day. How would he survive the entire house party?

When he'd ventured out this morning, he hadn't thought that any of them—let alone the one who plagued his thoughts—would be up at this early hour. Not only up, but exploring the grounds as if it was the most natural thing in the world for a beautiful young woman to do, and alone no less.

On a long, exasperated sigh he responded, "Shadow." With the mention of his name, the dog jumped up and went to where Damian was standing.

He patted his leg for Shadow to follow, then started to turn away, when she asked another question. "Do you often walk alone with him?"

"Yes. It is only me and Shadow. Now if you'll excuse us—"

"Would you mind company this morning?" Her words were sincere, not intrusive, as if she truly wanted to walk with them. But it simply could not be.

He looked heavenwards, hoping patience would be bestowed upon him. "It's not appropriate," he grumbled. Not that anyone would force her to marry an unseemly beast, but he would not jeopardize her reputation just the same. "I will escort you back to the house."

"Thank you," was all she said.

Much to Damian's relief, Miss Theodora did not ask any more questions on the short journey back. However, he could not escape the feeling that she was studying him out of the corner of her eye. It would be best for all if he kept his distance.

AFTER THEODORA RETURNED from her walk, she kept to her room and attempted to read until the day officially began. Her mind kept drifting to the interaction with Lord Grimsby. He seemed to want to be seen as a beastly sort of man, and yet, there was such a gentleness about him that made the former seem laughable.

"Thank you for the note. I had a feeling you would be up early," Evelina said as she entered the chamber and sat at the foot of the bed. "Did you enjoy your walk this morning?"

"Yes, very much so. I encountered Lord Grimsby and Shadow."

"Shadow?" Evelina questioned with a raised brow.

"His dog." Theodora liked the dog. She could tell that he was happy and playful, and utterly devoted to his master. It said a lot about a person to be able to inspire such affection in another living creature.

"That is an unusual name for a dog."

"I agree, but it suits him. I suspect he is never far from Lord Grimsby, just like a shadow trailing behind, keeping watch." Theodora stretched her limbs. "Do you know what is planned for today?"

Evelina said, "I do not. I was hoping we would have some time away from the mamas to converse with our friends." Although the sisters would not be able to discuss at liberty the things they wanted to, they each hoped that the opportunity would arise for them to share their personal thoughts and ideas with others. "Aunt Imogene was speaking with Lady Stanbourne at length last evening, perhaps she knows."

A short time later, her question was answered by Aunt Imogene as the trio made their way to the day parlor. "Lady Stanbourne mentioned last evening that since a couple of ladies and several gentlemen were still due to arrive today, the activities are to be more casual, with the main festivities beginning tomorrow. However, she did arrange for a friend of hers to sing this evening. From what Lady Stanbourne has said, Mrs. Roake is quite an accomplished soprano."

Theodora had always enjoyed such entertainments. She wondered if Lord Grimsby would be in attendance. From the snippets she'd gathered, she thought he was very fond of music.

As they neared the parlor, the sound of gleeful chatter rose. It was such a pleasant change from the numerous obligations and hectic schedule required in London. She felt much more herself in the country and was looking forward to exploring the grounds.

They took a seat nearest one of the large windows. Theodora had a hard time focusing on those around her as her eyes kept drifting to the landscape. She shifted her position, putting the temptation behind her.

Although the conversation was not very stimulating, she was enjoying the company surrounded by some friends. One of the mamas suggested a stroll, and that was all the encouragement Theodora and her sister needed. They both practically leapt from their seats, encouraging the others to not dally a moment longer.

The chatter continued as the ladies strolled from the parlor and into the lovely afternoon. Soon, small groups were formed. Theodora—although not wanting to exclude—was pleased that their group included Miss Ashton and Miss Raine, along with a new addition, Miss O'Donnell.

Once clear of their friends' chaperones, Theodora and her sister were much more at ease with the conversation. Aunt Imogene was the only older woman they trusted with their secrets. They walked down the gravel path, surrounded by immaculately sculpted topiaries.

"I do hope we will be able to have more opportunities such as this," Miss Ashton said with hope. "I miss our gatherings in London."

Theodora did, too, but not the city itself.

"We don't know how many opportunities we will have to meet while here, but if you ever find yourself in need of assistance, we"—Evelina paused as she glanced to Theodora, then continued—"devised a code. Just say *By Zeus*, and we will come to your aid."

It was a code the three sisters had used frequently while in Town, especially when cornered by naysayers and gossips. They'd once been criticized by Lady Mavis for being silly little children by using such a term. *Little did she know*, Theodora thought with an inward giggle.

"Any questions?" Theodora asked.

Worrying her hands, Miss Raine spoke first. "Of the gentlemen present, which ones should we be wary of?"

The other two friends present nodded their heads as if they'd been wondering the same.

"Fortunately, Lord Grimsby's aunt seems to keep good company, and all, except Lord Spalding and Mr. Leveson, are acceptable and have no scandal surrounding their names," Evelina responded.

It was only just that morning that Aunt Imogene had warned Theodora and Evelina that those two particular men—although quite charming—were known fortune hunters. However, in the end they had been wrong about Mr. Greenford in London, so perhaps they'd found themselves in a similar situation of inheriting a mountain of debt. But it was better to err on the side of caution.

"I do hope to secure a proposal by the end of the party," Miss O'Donnell sighed.

Miss Raine, with all her sweet innocence, said, "I didn't know you had your cap set at a particular gentleman."

"I don't," the lady responded with a giggle. "I am just ready to marry and be away from my sister's schemes. I truly do not know how much more I can take of her constant nagging about the color of my dresses or how my back isn't quite straight enough or that I do not smile enough in the presence of eligible gentlemen. It's all very tiring."

Miss O'Donnell was the youngest of five sisters, and with her mother's failing health, her eldest sister had taken over chaperoning duties. It was not the first time she'd complained about her sister, and Theodora suspected it wouldn't be the last.

Speaking with a wisdom beyond her years, Miss Ashton interjected, "Never settle because you want to run from your problems. That will only lead to more." Although Miss Ashton hadn't been running from her problems, she had almost found herself in the unfortunate situation of being married to a fortune hunter. Thankfully, her family discovered Mr. Markham's true intentions and put a stop to it before any damage was done to Miss Ashton's reputation.

"I can't imagine more problems. So many are plaguing my thoughts," Miss O'Donnell admitted.

"Like what?" Evelina questioned with concern.

"My mother won't discuss anything, and my sister . . ." Miss O'Donnell rolled her eyes before continuing. "Well, her explanation of things whenever I ask a question about"—she lowered her voice, then whispered—"*you know* is lacking at best. She just tells me it's my duty to provide an heir." She threw her hands up. "I know that! But what I don't know is how that is achieved."

"We all suffer the same complaint," Miss Raine commiserated.

Theodora was thankful that none present asked again what her and Evelina had learned from Alexandra. What their eldest sister revealed—which was not much—had been more puzzling than informative.

"And that is why we are here, to aid each other," Evelina said with a determination Theodora had not heard before. Of her two sisters, Evelina was more guarded with her thoughts. On more than one occasion she suspected Evelina was hiding something, perhaps too unsure of her own emotions to share.

The girls continued to enjoy the remainder of the afternoon in each other's company. It was such a pleasant change from the Season. It was nice to be surrounded by good friends whom one could trust.

THEODORA HAD VERY much been looking forward to this evening's musical entertainments all day. Not only was Mrs. Roake an accomplished soprano, but she was also a proficient pianist, which happened to be Theodora's favorite instrument by far. She could not explain the feeling she got while sitting at the splendid instrument, her fingers moving across the keys creating a vibrant sound that fed her muse.

Theodora eagerly followed the other guests toward the music room. Once inside, she noticed one corner, saturated in dimness. She suspected *if* Lord Grimsby were to join them this evening that would be where he'd stand. She wondered if his aunt made certain that there was always a corner reserved for him in the hope that he would attend. Why he insisted on hiding in the shadows was beyond her comprehension.

She'd seen him in daylight just that morning, and although he wore a mask that covered part of his face, she suspected the scarring was not that severe and that the scars on the inside were far greater. What had he suffered? Was he still carrying guilt?

As Mrs. Roake began to sing a beautiful Italian love song, accompanied by her husband on the pianoforte, so many other questions swept through her mind. By the time the performance came to an end, she was exhausted and out of sorts from all the wondering and speculation. She prayed that sleep would not evade her tonight.

Chapter Four

THE NEXT DAY brought much the same as previous days, the only difference being the abundance of guests. After overseeing delivery of food baskets to his tenants, Damian stayed sequestered in his study, claiming estate business, while his aunt played hostess and his cousin endured more social activities. The young lad was slowly coming into his own and becoming more comfortable with larger groups.

Every evening, Damian and Horatio would discuss the events of the day, go over any estate business, and make plans for future improvements on the estate. Part of their discussions included Damian reassuring Horatio in all matters of the earldom. Despite his insecurities, he was making huge strides in learning the business of being an earl.

Damian had wanted to attend last evening's musical entertainments, and Aunt Esther had assured him a corner would remain unlit, but after the reaction to his appearance on that first evening the guests had arrived, he decided it was best for all to remain hidden. At least for the time being, until his aunt forced him from the shadows, which, based on their argument early in the day, was quickly approaching.

Until then, he would enjoy the quiet solitude that was his curse and his comfort. At least he could watch the dining festivities from the narrow balcony and see how his cousin was fairing.

"Come on, Shadow, let's ready for dinner." Based on the fast-sweeping motion of his tail, Shadow knew it was time to eat. The animal was always ready for food.

"DO YOU THINK *he'll* be there?" Theodora whispered with hopefulness to her sister as they strolled toward the drawing room, trailing behind Aunt Imogene, who'd dashed ahead to speak with Lady Vernon.

Without hesitation, her sister responded, "No."

"No? That was rather firm, Evelina." Theodora knew there was little chance of Lord Grimsby joining them this evening, of course. He hadn't joined the party since the evening of the first night, but she still could hope.

Evelina stopped and faced her. "He does not make appearances at these events. It's as if he were a phantom in his own home." She tilted her head and studied Theodora for a moment. She knew that encouraging gleam in her sister's eyes even before the words exited her mouth. "Perhaps you need to search him out."

Perhaps.

Laughter echoed down the hall, signaling most guests had already arrived. When they entered the opulent pale green and gold space, their suspicions were confirmed. Everyone—save one—was in attendance.

No sooner had the sisters entered the room than Miss Raine came rushing up to them, with a wide smile on her face.

"He's here," she murmured with excited panic. It was clear that a gentleman had caught their friend's attention.

Evelina leaned in and whispered, "Who's here?"

Theodora followed the direction of Miss Raine's eyes, while

trying to not look too obvious. "Mr. Malone?"

Miss Raine nodded her head enthusiastically as she worried her hands. "What do I do? Should I try to speak with him? But then what do I say?"

Now was not the place to have this conversation, not with Mrs. Raine—Miss Raine's aunt—watching so closely. Still, she didn't want to ignore the request.

Only two words escaped her mouth before she was interrupted. "You could—"

"Daisy, I require you," Miss Raine's aunt scolded from a dozen paces away.

Theodora did not know if the chaperone objected to her and Evelina or just objected in general. From what Aunt Imogene had shared with the sisters earlier about the guests in attendance, Theodora suspected it was the latter. Mrs. Raine had married the youngest brother of the late Lord Raine. The only thing she enjoyed in life—according to Aunt Imogene—was the wealth she'd married into and laudanum. She was of the same ilk as the Dowager Viscountess Raine. Neither was agreeable. However, Miss Daisy Raine was the complete antithesis of the two elder women in her family. She was sincere and pleasant and was quickly becoming one of their closest friends.

Thankfully for Miss Raine, she did not have to endure her aunt for long. Dinner was soon called, and she was paired with a gentleman who her aunt at least somewhat approved of based on the smaller scowl she wore.

With all the couples finally lined up, they strolled to the banquet hall. The previous dinners had been held in the small dining room, but Lady Stanbourne had informed them that now that all the guests had arrived, the banquet hall was more suitable.

Conversation swirled as they paraded toward their destination, but Theodora was too preoccupied with the awe and splendor of this part of the house to participate. At some point during the course of the day, the main hall had been filled with a colorful display of hothouse flowers. She'd seen much of the house when Lady Stanbourne had given the tour, but tonight, there seemed to be a difference that she had difficulty identifying. Perhaps it was the fragrant scent of flowers that drifted through the air, or that everyone was in attendance, or maybe simply the sparkle of the candlelight that reflected in the large windows. But whatever it was, she found it most appealing.

As she entered the opulent banquet hall, her attention instantly turned to the *trompe l'oeil* of an ancient city that spanned the length of the room on one side. She followed the painted columns as they stretched upward two stories, capped with a Corinthian motif. Her gaze instantly shifted to a small, narrow balcony, framed by a painted trellis with climbing vines gracing one corner of the room. It was so narrow, in fact, one might easily miss it entirely.

That's odd. Why would there be a balcony inside overlooking the dining table?

Before her mind could wrap itself around the oddity of the narrow opening on the second-floor corner, everyone took their seats and the meal service began.

The exceptionally long table had been laid out with lovely blue and white Wedgwood china, crystal glasses, and an enticing aromatic first course. In the center was a beautiful arrangement of flowers similar to those adorning the house. It was an elegant display of food and wealth, but not pretentious in the least.

Lady Stanbourne sat at the top of the table with the Marquess of Dufferin on her right and the Earl of Carrick on her left, while Mr. Eastwick sat at the bottom flanked by Lady Dufferin and Lady Vernon. Theodora had been paired with Lord Spalding, who was quite talkative this evening.

Throughout the meal, Theodora could not escape the feeling that someone was watching from above, but every time she glanced up toward the balcony, no one was there. It must be her overactive imagination.

"Are you enjoying the country?" Lord Spalding questioned. "It is a pleasant change from all the social requirements of

London. Do you prefer Town or the country?"

"I enjoy the country and long walks much more than the crowded streets of London." She would like to be taking a long stroll at this very moment, or sitting at the piano, losing herself in music. It had been far too long since she'd last indulged.

"I do prefer the country as well, but I am not fond of walking," Lord Spalding admitted. "I would much rather be racing my curricle." He took a bite of fish, then with a mouthful of food added, "Of course, speed is dependent on weather and the state of the roads."

Why did every topic seem to center on weather and roads? Wasn't this mundane conversation exactly what the Grace sisters had been trying to avoid during the Season? How easy it was to digress to what was deemed as acceptable—however dull it may be—rather than engage in stimulating, intellectual conversation. Perhaps men like Lord Spalding did not believe women capable of such discussions. And that was precisely why Theodora intended to avoid marrying a man such as he.

Out of the corner of her eye, she spied Evelina, practically pleading for help. Clearly her dinner partner was just as unstimulating as her own. And the evening was only just beginning. One thing was for certain, the sisters would have plenty to discuss once in the privacy of their rooms this evening.

FROM DAMIAN'S VANTAGE point, it looked as if the dinner party was a success. The food looked splendid, guests were smiling, and even his cousin appeared at ease. There was only one problem . . .

Miss Theodora Grace.

He stopped counting how many times she glanced upward to this balcony, which could hardly be called that in his estimation. It was more like a narrow glassless window that overlooked the room below.

Legend had it that his great-great grandfather had this slot in the wall created when he could no longer maneuver the stairs in his old age. Not trusting his younger wife to entertain on her own, he ordered for the opening to be added and would watch as she hosted dinner parties, then later give his critique on what she could improve upon. Toward the end of his life, his wife stopped entertaining and spent each mealtime with her husband, seeing to his every comfort and need.

When Damian and his brother were children, it was always great fun to sneak out of the nursery and watch their parents entertain. But he hadn't stood at this opening since long before the tragedy. As a child, he'd never imagined that he would use this vantage point himself to spy, simply to feel as if he were somewhat part of the world.

He spied Miss Theodora Grace glancing upward yet again. What did she hope to see? Did she hope to catch a glimpse of him? Was it morbid curiosity or did she feel the same pull that he been experiencing since their first meeting in London?

Laughter and gaiety drifted upward, teasing him, mocking him. He turned from the balcony and rested his head against the cool wall. How he longed to be surrounded by family and friends, to feel love again. As if reading his thoughts, Shadow nuzzled against his leg. He leaned down and stroked his soft, thick fur. "Thank you, ol' boy." Did his four-legged companion realize just how much he meant to Damian?

Time passed and the meal concluded. Once the ladies adjourned to the drawing room, Damian continued to keep watch and listen to the men as they took brandy and conversed. Apart from a couple of obligatory invites, the gentlemen Aunt Esther had decided upon were not the rowdy rakes about Town but were chosen to compliment the number of ladies. His aunt had been most particular with the guest list. As the minutes ticked, he was thankful there was no talk of him, only of the hunt that was to take place two days hence.

As the evening progressed, he found himself more and more

agitated. He was not used to having so many people in residence, restricting his movements within his own home. Desperate for a moment to himself, he moved through the house toward the small private music room, used not for entertaining but for his own musical purpose. As he entered the room, warmth brushed past him and moonlight caressed the walls. He shut the door to the outside world. This was where he spent his evenings. This was where his soul found some semblance of solace.

Shadow dashed into the room, going to his favorite spot beside the fireplace, circled several times, let out a long moan, then curled up on the rug, perfectly content.

Damian knew he was not going to find contentment so quickly. He strolled to the large piano, his only true comfort. Once his fingers touched the ivory keys, he could feel the music surging from within. A part of him came to life, and the worries and pain from the past dissipated somewhat, and the serenity that came from his music flowed out through his hands, filling the room. But even with the joy of his music, he was anxious.

NOT FOR THE first time in her life—and certainly it wouldn't be the last—Theodora found herself unable to sleep. When she was little, she'd feared the darkness and the strange sounds that accompanied it, but when her dearest papa took ill, and she'd vowed to be with him during the dark night hours, she discovered a peacefulness lurking in the shadows. There was nothing to fear, for within the darkness Theodora could lose herself to her imagination, to the possibilities, without censure from the outside world.

And so, she found herself wandering Grimsby Hall, hoping to find solace in the library. Now if she could just remember the direction . . .

The faint chords of a sonata drifted down the hall, calling to her heart. Theodora moved toward the sound, pulled by some unseen force. It was such a sad melody, but so beautiful just the same. She followed the sound in a dreamlike trance, wondering who could bring forth such a beautiful sound from the pianoforte. As she neared the closed door, she moved quietly and carefully so as not to startle whoever was inside. She leaned against the wall beside the door and just listened as the music emanated through it. But she was curious as to who was playing, and at this late hour.

She lifted her hand, reaching for the knob, her mind warning that perhaps she should not disturb the occupant, but her heart insisted otherwise. Ever so softly, her hand wrapped around the cool knob and turned it. She had only edged the door open an inch when the music filled her, sending hundreds of tingles coursing through her body, bringing it to life. Without thought, she entered the room, wanting to feel more of the delectable sound. A small candelabra on a side table and glowing embers from the fireplace were the only light in the room, adding to the air of mystery.

All of a sudden, the music stopped, and an angry voice stormed from the dimness beyond, replacing the tones that had been invigorating her soul. "What are you doing here?"

She instantly knew whose voice that was.

"Lord Grimsby, I apologize, but I could not sleep." Before she could plead her case further, Shadow got up, stretched his limbs, and came to her side. "Well, hello there. And how are you this evening?" she said as she stroked his soft head.

Although Lord Grimsby was just a silhouette in the distance, she could see that he reached for his mask. As he placed it on his face, he scolded, "And you thought it acceptable to wander the house?"

"Not wander with ill intention, I assure you." She held her ground as she continued to lavish attention on the dog. "You did tell me that there were plenty of places inside the house to pass the hours."

"Do you have no care for propriety?" he grumbled.

"We're only talking, and I trust you." Lord Grimsby's mouth opened and closed as if he was about to argue, but before he could, she added, "Shadow may be my chaperone for the evening." She stroked the dog's large head. "Isn't that right?" She then turned and addressed her reason for being there. "I was searching for the library when I heard music. You play quite well."

"Do not come any farther." His tone brooked no argument, but the downward slope of his shoulders suggested he was in need of friendship.

Theodora knew from tending to her father to take time and have patience. There was something about Damian that called to her—had from the very first meeting. She could have patience. For a little while at least.

"May I stand here and listen to you play?"

Her question seemed to catch him off guard, but he quickly regained himself. "You really should retire before—"

"Please?"

No sooner had the word brushed past her lips than he began to play that soulful sonata once again. The tender chords, soft as a lover's touch, reached her core, caressing her entire being. She closed her eyes as she inhaled the music, filling her senses with the sweet intoxication of the notes he played. She was utterly lost in the moment.

And then the music decrescendoed, coming to a gentle end. She opened her eyes to find Lord Grimsby staring at her. She didn't want to ruin the moment with words of praise that she was certain he would find uncomfortable. He didn't seem to take well to compliments. Perhaps he found them forced. But she didn't want to just leave, and so she settled on simple politeness.

"Thank you," she offered, then took her leave, hoping he felt the sincerity of her words.

WHAT HAD JUST happened?

One moment he'd been lost in his music, and the next, exposing a part of his soul that he'd locked away to protect it from the painful past. And in the breath of a single word, *please*, he'd abandoned his fears and played for Theodora.

The sight of her as she closed her eyes, gently swaying to the music—his music—was the most intoxicating he'd ever beheld. She brought life to the notes he played, the sound he created. His heart ached to watch her longer. There was a gentle pureness, yet intense strength, about her that he was drawn to.

Bloody hell, but he needed to keep his distance. He was hosting this house party to secure a countess for his cousin, not torment himself with what could never be. During the day, it was simple enough to hide and not interact. The guests preferred it that way. Who would want to spend time with a scarred beast?

The trouble was at night when his body was too restless to sleep and his mind was being assailed by the past. His music had been his saving grace through the years, and in one evening Theodora had disrupted his senses and given him a hope he was certain he'd never experienced. Her caring smile and . . .

Stop thinking about her!

Perhaps he should remove to one of the cottages on the estate for the duration of the gathering. He could join certain festivities during the day, then retreat once everyone retired. Aunt Esther would be certain to disapprove, and he would probably never hear the end of it. However, keeping his distance was essential to ensuring he wouldn't suffer a broken heart.

Again.

Chapter Five

WHILE AUNT ESTHER was busy readying everyone for the afternoon's event on the south lawn, Damian watched from the veranda. Perched high to observe, but not partake.

He was pleased that Horatio appeared at ease today, almost as if he was enjoying the role of host. Horatio had yet to mention any particular young lady that he was interested in, but Damian could not help but wonder if some of his confidence stemmed from a desire to show himself capable of running the earldom.

Damian watched as Horatio strolled toward another group of ladies, including the Grace sisters.

Miss Theodora Grace.

How enticingly beautiful she appeared today with her rich auburn hair glistening in the afternoon sunlight, reminding him of a vibrant autumn sunset. Even from this distance he could feel the warmth in her smile as she enjoyed the company of those around her. And then Theodora glanced his way, her eyes settling on him, and her smile softened.

What was she thinking?

Hope coursed through his veins for the briefest of moments before reality thundered down upon him.

She probably pities you, like everyone else.

How could he ever expect more? It was all he had known

since the tragedy. But why then could he not stop thinking about her?

"Pardon me, Lord Grimsby," Howard, his butler, said, interrupting the ponderings that plagued him. "Lady Stanbourne has requested your presence at the treasure hunt."

"Of course she has," he mumbled for his ears only. He sucked in his breath and spoke over his shoulder. "You may tell my aunt that I am perfectly content watching the festivities from here."

"Lady Stanbourne thought you might say as much and . . . and asked me to relay . . ." Howard cleared his throat and continued in a less than confident tone, "that it is your duty to attend these activities."

Damn his aunt. She should not be putting his butler in such a position. He was about to say so when Howard stepped to his side and added, "I have known you since the day you were born. It is time you rejoined the living." And with that, he left Damian alone with his thoughts.

Leave it to Howard to be so forthcoming in his opinions. He was always one to speak his mind, and through the years, Damian had appreciated his honesty. He was a great asset to the estate and had kept things running smoothly even in the darkest of times. He'd been counting on the faithful butler to aid Horatio when the time came. But now . . . the murky depths of uncertainty started to give way to a faint stream of possibilities.

His pulse raced and he felt as if his world was starting to spiral. All he wanted was to secure the earldom, and yet at every turn, someone was disrupting his plans. Sucking in a deep breath, he looked heavenward and let out a long, deep sigh. Damian supposed one afternoon in daylight would not be too terrible.

"Come on, Shadow. Let's be good hosts." The dog seemed to need no further encouragement as he dashed off in the direction of the guests.

Although his mask was fastened, concealing the scars that marred his face, he was acutely aware of the stares from those present. He spied his aunt in the near distance and knew he must stay the course, and so he continued. As he got nearer, several of the ladies eyed him with a mixture of pity and alarm, a couple turning away, averting their gaze.

How much more did he have to endure before he could retreat and hide once again?

No sooner had the thought formed in his mind, than his aunt approached, concern lacing her features.

"I see you received my message," she said under her breath. "Thank you for coming."

"You shouldn't have put Howard in that position."

"We will discuss this later," was all his aunt said on the subject before she turned to their guests. "Now that Lord Grimsby has joined us, it's time for the hunt. Everyone has their list and team." She waved her hands wide and announced, "Go and explore!"

ALTHOUGH SHE WANTED to stay behind and converse with Lord Grimsby, Theodora was ecstatic at the prospect of exploring the grounds. Except for the one morning walk and the few all-too-brief strolls with the other ladies, she had yet to see much of the gardens or beyond.

"Are you to join our party?" Lord Neave said as he looked past Theodora.

Her heart skipped a beat as she turned around and came face to face with Lord Grimsby.

"I think the first clue is leading us in this direction," Miss Raine called. "What do you think Lord Neave?"

"Excuse me, Grimsby," Lord Neave said with a slight nod of his head, then turned his attention to Miss Raine.

The elusive earl nodded his head but did not make eye contact.

"Good afternoon, Lord Grimsby," Theodora greeted.

Keeping his eyes diverted from her, with a nod of his head, he said, "Good afternoon, Miss Theodora." Then looked as if he was going to turn away.

Desperate to have more of a conversation, Theodora blurted the first question that came to mind. "And are you enjoying the festivities?" She inwardly shook her head. He hadn't participated in any so how could he enjoy them? What must he think of her?

However, his response held no disdain for her question. Quite the contrary. Pride over his relative's efforts was evident in his words. "My aunt has done a wonderful job."

"Yes, she has." This was becoming the longest conversation they'd had, and she didn't want it to end. "I particularly enjoyed Mrs. Roake's performance. I've always found songs in Italian quite emotional."

His eyes met hers, lovely blue eyes with such warmth and kindness. "I agree," he whispered, almost in confusion, as if their shared opinion was disrupting him.

She wanted to discover more about his musical interests, how long he'd been playing, who were his favorite composers. She just wanted to know him.

Theodora was about to ask another question, one about the piece he'd played, when Lord Neave called to her. "Are you coming Miss Theodora? Miss Raine has figured out the location of the first clue."

"You best join your party. Good day, Miss Theodora," he said, then he turned and went toward where his aunt was talking with a couple of the mamas.

Theodora would have rather stayed and conversed about music, but she knew not to press. There would be another opportunity to discuss all things related to music. She would make certain of that.

She picked up her pace and joined the pair, but she'd taken no more than a dozen steps when Shadow appeared at her side. "Would you like to join us?" she cooed as she greeted the dog with a pat of his head. The dog seemed content to stay by her side, for the time being at least. She welcomed the companionship. It had been too long since she'd had a dog of her own.

Their first clue had taken them to a statue of the goddess Hera in the Italian garden. She was standing larger than life, full of confidence, and wearing a crown, a veil draped about her body. A rolled paper scroll was tucked into a space at her feet.

Theodora unwound the sheaf and before she had a chance to read it, Miss Raine with bubbly excitement asked, "What does it say?"

"You can still enjoy these even when the easterly wind blows." Theodora glanced up from the paper and thought a moment. "The next clue must be in the Orangery."

No sooner had the words left her lips, than Miss Raine was dashing off down the pathway, past a small reflecting pool surrounded by topiaries. "I believe Miss Raine is determined to win the treasure hunt," Lord Neave said with a chuckle.

"I agree!" She looked down to Shadow and said, "Come on, let's go find the next clue."

As they neared the Orangery, a loud chirping sound caught Shadow's attention. He stopped in his tracks and looked about, deciding which direction the sound came from. A moment later, he took off in the direction they'd just come from, barking at the unforeseen threat. Theodora inwardly chuckled. Her own precious Thalia had been just the same. Sadness weighed in her heart. She missed her childhood pet, missed the unconditional love and sweet companionship her pup had offered through the years.

Theodora was impressed by the sheer size of the Orangery. A few minutes later, the trio entered the warm space. A rich, earthy scent wafted through the air followed by a hint of sweetness. Remembrances of the Orangery at her childhood home drifted through her musings. She inhaled deeply, trying to identify the intoxicating aromas filling the hothouse.

"Another clue!" Miss Raine's excitement echoed off the glass startling Theodora. "Over here, Miss Theodora."

Theodora followed the sound of her friend's voice past a row of lemon trees. She wondered if Lord Grimsby also grew pineapples. They were certainly a peculiar looking fruit. That was another topic she could discuss with him. She filed that in her mind for another time. Soon, she was standing amongst an assortment of tropical plants.

"I think this clue is directing us to the reflecting pond," Lord Neave stated as Theodora approached.

And before she could put two words together, Miss Raine was dashing ahead of them. "Let's hurry!"

The afternoon passed in a flurry of rushing to find clues. What felt like hours later, they had finally completed the list and were walking back to where Lady Stanbourne waited with some of the mamas.

Although her team was the first to gather all the clues, Theodora's heart sank when she did not see Lord Grimsby or his dog. Theodora was so curious about the man. Would he ever stop avoiding people? How could she get through to him?

DAMIAN STOOD BY the window, staring out into the dark night, trying to focus on the serene calm and the beautiful moon illuminating the sleeping landscape, and not his reflection or, worse, the mask he wore.

He'd survived the treasure hunt, though in truth he hadn't joined in, and as soon as all the players scattered to find their clues, he'd retreated to his study. And there he'd stayed for the remainder of the day and into the evening. He'd sent word to his aunt that he was consumed with estate business that required his immediate attention. He knew the excuse was getting tiresome and that it was wearing thin with his aunt. In truth, Grimsby Hall and his other properties were all running smoothly and prospering, but he had no other reason to offer, besides the fact that he did not want to participate.

Without a knock, the door to his study opened, then closed with a firm click. He knew, without a doubt, his aunt had come to lecture, scold, or try to convince him he was being unreasonable. Perhaps all three. He turned and came face to face with his irate aunt. It would definitely be all three.

Shadow—having only looked up to see who the intruder was at this hour—was completely unconcerned with the arrival of Aunt Esther.

"I require a word with you," she said with annoyance as she stood on the other side of the desk.

"Only one?"

"Words," his relative said, emphasizing the last letter. She didn't wait for a response but went straight into her grievances. "This has gone on long enough. You are not making an effort to get to know our guests, and you need to make an appearance at least at a few of the activities."

"I have been present—"

Aunt Esther crossed her arms. "Yes. After dinner on the first evening, but only for a brief time, *and* you kept to the darkest corner of the room. And then at the treasure hunt this afternoon, for which I had to have Howard retrieve you, *but* you did not participate. You practically ran off as soon as the guests went searching for clues. You are the host—"

"I asked for your assistance so I wouldn't have to attend." He ran a frustrated hand through his hair. Why was this becoming so complicated? He had an aunt who was being difficult, a cousin who didn't want to inherit the earldom, and a dog who was forever running off with the one woman he definitely should not be thinking about! Why couldn't those in his life just accept his decision and make things as simple as possible?

"No. You asked for my assistance so you could hide, not only physically, but emotionally." Clearly, Aunt Esther was not going to consider making things simple. She took in a deep, frustrated breath, then started anew. "Well, I care about you too much to let you do so any longer. I did not interfere when you sent your sister to live with me, but I will not have another regret hanging over my head."

Hurt ripped through his heart and settled into the pit of his stomach. "You regret taking in Theresa?"

"Absolutely not!" Those two words his aunt spoke eased some of the pain he'd just experienced. "She was such a joy and brightened many a day."

As the hurt eased, a desire to understand grew. "Then what regret did you have?"

Aunt Esther's tone turned melancholy, sorrowful. "That I did not help her with what she was feeling, her thoughts and emotions over losing her parents, her eldest brother, and . . . *you*."

"She didn't lose me, she—"

"The day you sent her to live with me, she did lose you." Tears glistened in Aunt Esther's eyes. "She loved you dearly, but was afraid—"

"Of the way I looked." He turned away, years of sorrow and pain pressed against his chest. "I know."

"No." The single word was firm, insistent.

He whipped around and faced her. "Then what?" His voice grew louder with each word he spoke. "What was she afraid of?" Why was his relative speaking in riddles?

"She was afraid of being turned away . . ." Her words trailed and sadness filled her eyes. "From you."

"Why would I—?"

Her shoulders drooped as she blinked away the tears that were pooling in the corner of her eyes. "After your mother died, you sent her to live with me and never visited."

Remorse wrapped its tenacious arms about his heart as his dear sister's cries echoed in his mind. "She could not stand to look at me. What was I supposed to do? I wanted to give her a better life. A happier life."

Aunt Esther came around the desk and stood next to him. She put a gentle hand on his arm as she said, "Theresa has a happy life, but she misses her brother tremendously. Ever since the tragedy, you've pushed everyone who cares about you away. That is your greatest mistake."

Guilt weighed heavy in his gut. Had he been so wrong in his understanding of those events? No, he remembered it all with too much clarity—his sister's cries, his mother's wails. It still haunted his nights.

He was about to argue when his relative squeezed his arm to keep his attention, then offered advice. "Stop running from the past. You tried to save them, but you cannot change what happened. It was not your fault." Her tone softened. "What you can change are the mistakes of the past that continue in your present." And with that, she left the room, leaving him alone with his thoughts.

His present.

He could make an appearance at the various activities, but that wouldn't change the fact that he was a beast, a scarred monster who frightened women and children. The fire may not have been his fault, but if he'd only arrived sooner, if only he hadn't been delayed, he could have saved them all.

After his aunt left, Damian stood by the window, once again trying not to reflect on the past. He strategized about improvements for the Orangery, adding another block to the stables, trying to focus on anything but the past. But thoughts of his sister plagued him.

Had he been mistaken in his actions with her?

He went to his desk and pulled out the letters she'd sent him. She'd never asked to return home, but after his aunt's revelation he reread some of the correspondence. A fierce pain struck his heart, suffocating past beliefs. It was true that Theresa never asked to come home—not specifically—not in so many words, but in every letter, she asked about her horse, the staff, the garden—how did it look, were the roses in bloom. He'd always responded to letters, but he never asked her to come home. Never asked if she wanted to return to Grimsby Hall. Years' worth of regrets roiled within. He was at a complete loss as to what to do.

By the time he retired to the earl's chamber, Damian was beyond exhausted. But as he drifted off to sleep the events from the past that he'd fought so hard to keep from his mind stormed their way forward.

Deafening sounds of cracking timber echoed all around.

"Papa!" he called. "John!" he yelled. But neither his father nor his brother answered back.

He promised himself he would not give up until he found them, even as heat pressed against his body, filling his lungs. He would not give up. Raising his arm, he covered his nose and mouth in the crook of his elbow as he plunged farther into the inferno.

A faint moan rose above the sound of crackling debris. Damian fell to the floor, ignoring the pain searing through his body, and he crawled toward the sound.

"Papa?" His throat burned as the single word ached from his mouth. He pulled himself toward his father's trapped body.

He started to lift the beam when Father's weak hand rested on his. "Go . . . go to . . ." The hoarse words were strangled on a cough. Then with one last breath, his sire forced a word past his lips. "John."

Panic gripped him. "John!" he screamed over and over as he searched for his brother. Hot embers rained down upon him, singeing his clothes, but he was determined to find his only brother.

A loud crack resounded overhead. He looked up just as one of the beams started to disintegrate. Damian ran as the structure around him began to collapse, but he would not leave John behind. He would find his brother.

"Damian . . ."

John.

An unseen force pulled at him. Seconds, perhaps minutes passed as he crawled through what once was the hunting lodge, clawing at whatever could aid him in moving forward.

"Damian . . ."

He wouldn't give up. He couldn't. He had to find . . .

Damian bolted upright, drenched in sweat, his heart pounding against his chest as he fought for breath. He rubbed a hand across his unmasked face, feeling the ridges of the scars that marred the right side of his face.

It was just a nightmare.

Why wouldn't the past let him rest? He'd tried to save his father and brother, but the flames had been too much for a mere mortal. Hadn't he suffered enough?

Night after night during his recovery, he'd swallowed his own cries of pain because of his mother's sorrow over losing her husband and firstborn son. Far too often, her wails had echoed down the hall, settling into his soul. Those tormented cries of love lost still haunted him.

But Damian's suffering had only just begun.

And then his suffering had worsened with the arrival of his fiancée—the woman he'd thought shared his love. But she'd only offered a glance his way, then turned in horror and left him. Left him because she could not stand the sight of him.

Damian remembered that distant day with all too much clarity.

As with most who entered his room, he had been pretending to sleep. He hadn't yet had the energy to talk to anyone, to face the demons that had been plaguing him since he had first awoken after the fire. As she'd neared the bed, her words were loud and shockingly clear. *Good Lord, he's a beast of a monster.* She'd run from the room and from his life.

After that dreadful night, he'd donned his first mask, a covering made of silk with slits for his eyes, nose, and mouth. Once he was strong enough, he'd consulted a tanner and leatherworker and began to experiment with his own creations. It gave him something useful to do while the world of the living passed him by. He spent months perfecting a half-mask that would hide the ugliness. But it was not enough.

Even with the half-mask that hid the scars, people whispered and children cried. As the years passed, the whispers hadn't diminished. All sorts of rumors emerged about the man he'd become. He could not ignore them, and so he retreated further into himself, indulging in his music, tending to various types of plants growing in the Orangery, and ensuring the earldom was prospering. He owed the latter to his father and eldest brother. His current course was for the best.

The sooner his cousin chose his bride and the house party was done, the better.

Chapter Six

THE PAIN OF the past was often too much to bear. Damian was anxious and agitated, his soul in agony. But tonight, there was something else plaguing him as well. Something he couldn't define with words. The intensity of the unseen force pressing against his chest was worse than he'd ever felt. What was wrong with him? Why couldn't he be at peace?

At times such as this, music was his only solace. Perhaps that would help ease what was roiling within. Without wasting another moment, he changed his clothes and went in search of peace.

He wandered through the house, attempting to enjoy the quiet stillness of night, toward his private music room at the far end of the house. Far away from guests and prying eyes.

As he neared his music room, the restlessness in his body surged into his fingers. He ached to play the piano, to create beautiful sounds, to escape.

He was only a dozen steps away when the chords of a sonata drifted past the slightly ajar door. The sound pulled him toward the opening. Who would dare be so bold as to enter his private space? He pushed the door wide to confront the trespasser, and he saw her.

Theodora.

She didn't look over toward him, but he was certain she knew he was there. She simply continued to play the most enticing sonata he'd ever heard. He stepped closer, completely mesmerized by her serene presence. The passion on her face as she lost herself to the music touched a part of him that he'd thought had died. There were simply no words for what he felt, what surged through his body. And in that moment, he knew he'd lost his heart to her.

What was he going to do?

He couldn't bare his soul to her, let her see the scars. She would turn in horror. That much he was certain of.

No. The best thing to do was to walk away, to keep his distance. Soon, she would marry someone who deserved her caring spirit. It was not him. Nothing he touched remained whole. He had not been able to save his father or brother. His mother had suffered night after night for over a year before she'd died of a broken heart. And his sister . . . his beautiful little sister . . . Damian had pushed her away, believing that he was doing the right thing, that he was protecting her. Now a cordial letter once a year was all that remained of their communication. But at least she was happily married to an Italian count, with a family of her own, and living on the continent. It was all for the best.

He sucked in a deep breath. His mind was made up. He whipped around and fled from the room. Theodora would thank him later.

THEODORA HAD BARELY slept after the encounter with Lord Grimsby last night—or Damian, as she couldn't help but think of him. He had watched as she played the piano, but he hadn't said a word. She had felt the torment warring within, and yet, he wouldn't speak. And then he'd gone.

Too ill at ease, she continued to play until the early hours. When the sun was just about to make an appearance and the servants would rise, only then did she retire. But sleep still evaded her. When it finally did come, it wasn't a restful sleep. No, quite the contrary. Theodora did not remember what she'd dreamt about, but when she woke, it was with a heavy heart and a pounding headache. She informed her aunt and sister that she was feeling under the weather and did not want to attend that day's picnic. Thankfully, neither protested.

After a soothing hot bath, followed by a meal in her room, she was feeling much more herself. Holding true to form, a couple of hours later, Theodora was tired of being cooped up in her room. She was never one to sit and lounge for any length of time and was ready to explore.

The guests were not due back from the picnic and lawn games for at least another hour or two. Plenty of time to indulge her curiosity without having to be social.

Grabbing her shawl, she left the room with no particular destination in mind. The house was calm, quiet. She strolled down the bright gallery, gazing out across the landscape. The house was very nicely situated with an abundance of natural light streaming into the various spaces. It was quite the opposite of the man who hid in darkness.

As she strolled past the drawing room, through the Marble Hall, toward the Tapestry room, something struck her as odd. She stopped and glanced about, then retraced her steps. She peered into the drawing room, then ventured to the other common areas, then to another side gallery. She must have been walking for nearly half an hour, trying to determine what was plaguing her. There was something missing in the drawing and reception rooms and hallways. And then it struck her. There were no mirrors. There were no mirrors visible in his London residence either.

The suite of rooms she shared with her aunt and sister had two mirrors. She assumed the other bedchambers also had mirrors or she was certain that one of the ladies in attendance would have protested by now, what with so many of them trying to make themselves appear like perfection for the sole purpose of attracting Mr. Eastwick's attention.

Had Lord Grimsby removed them because of his scars? Did he wander the house without a mask when no guests were present?

She strolled down the long gallery, admiring the paintings of the Grimsby ancestors that were hung between the doorways that led to other parts of the house. She could see his resemblance to the generations of Grimsby men before him, but she was more interested the gallery itself.

It was an impressive space with two fireplaces and multiple groupings of seating, allowing for guests to sit and enjoy the sunlight that filtered into the space. It was serene and peaceful. A lovely place to pass some time. She went to the window, gazing across the landscape, lost in her thoughts, when all of a sudden something rubbed against her leg. She looked down at the large dog at her side.

"Good afternoon, Shadow." The dog wagged its tail at her greeting, clearly waiting for her to shower him with affection. He did have a one-track mind at times, but she didn't mind. She enjoyed his company.

"I see you are roaming once again," Lord Grimsby said, standing in the dimness of a doorway across from her. His features were unreadable, but his voice didn't hold as much annoyance as on previous occasions.

"Never with ill intentions, I assure you. I just didn't feel like joining the others. Sometimes one just needs . . . solitude." Theodora bit the inside of her cheek. She didn't want to ramble— something she wasn't prone to do normally—but she didn't know what to talk about, and she certainly didn't want him to leave.

"I understand that," he said *sotto voce*.

His honest comment, which she was certain she wasn't meant to hear, took her aback for a moment. And then without thought, the words escaped her mouth. "Why do you hide in shadows?"

It looked as if he was about to retreat down the corridor from which he was standing, but then much to her surprise, he answered. "My appearance tends to startle people."

She suspected it was only part of the reason. "You cannot be as awful as you believe yourself to be."

He stepped from the threshold and into the gallery. Only a step, but it was enough for her to see his features—at least those not covered by his mask. There was nothing startling or even shocking about his appearance. Yes, he was tall, and very well-built, but there was a gentleness about him. She could see it in his eyes.

His left brow raised as he questioned, "And what drew you to that conclusion?"

Her response was simple. "Your dog."

"My dog? Shadow?" With the mention of his name, Shadow left her side and went to Damian's.

"Yes. I read in a story once that dogs are excellent judges of character, and yours clearly adores you." Just as the words left her mouth, Shadow nuzzled against Damian's leg, and let out a long, happy sigh, proving Theodora's point. "You see? Shadow is content by your side."

"Perhaps Shadow is wrong." *Perhaps you're wrong.* His unspoken words hung in the air between them.

"He's not wrong. Neither am I. And I intend to prove it to you." And with that, Theodora took her leave, leaving him standing there, just as he had left her the night before. Leaving him to ponder her words. One way or another, she would get through to him. She just wasn't certain how quite yet.

Theodora took her time returning to her room. No matter how hard she tried, she could not come up with a solution on how to reach Damian. Didn't he realize she wanted to offer friendship?

Some time later, she entered the suite she shared with her relatives, deciding to spend the remainder of the afternoon reading, when Evelina rushed in, completely out of sorts.

"Whatever is the matter?" She eyed her sister, but except for flushed features, she appeared intact. "Did something happen at the picnic?"

Evelina took in a long breath, then on the exhale, began her ramble. "The picnic was perfection. Everyone was pleasant. The weather was ideal, the food was excellent, and Lady Stanbourne is the perfect hostess." Something was amiss.

"Then whatever is the matter?" Clearly something had upset her sister.

"It's all changing, isn't it?" Evelina's words were tinged with sadness.

Theodora wasn't comprehending why her sister was so upset. "What is?"

"Life and . . ." Her elder sister shrugged her shoulders, then on a loud sigh she began her ramblings anew. "Oh, I don't know . . . everything! Alexandra is married. Miss Raine has hinted at an attachment. Miss O'Donnell and Miss Ashton have set their caps on undisclosed gentlemen, and you've formed a *tendre* for Lord Grimsby and—"

"How do you know that?" Theodora could not keep the shock from her voice. She'd been very guarded with her feelings, not really even accepting them herself, especially since the gentleman in question was being so reclusive. Though ever since she first spied him in London, she'd wanted to know him. The kindness in his eyes reached out to her, and the music he played infiltrated the most intimate of her thoughts and desires.

Her sister eyed her with disbelief. "Oh really, Theodora, I would have to be blind not to notice the way you look at him and blush whenever his name is mentioned. Ever since London it has been this way, and it has only increased since being here in the country. And it's clear that you are fond of his dog, as well."

Had she been so transparent? "Do you think anyone else realizes?"

"Luckily for you, Lord Grimsby does not attend many of the activities, and the ones he does attend are usually in the evening, so I think it has gone without notice. And besides, most of the mamas would discredit it any way. No one would believe a beautiful lady could be interested in—"

"Do not say the *beast*." Theodora detested that moniker, just as much as *The Phantom of Grimsby Hall*. He was neither. He was an admirable man of flesh and blood, who had tried to save his family. Why was the world so cruel about his appearance?

"I was not about to." Evelina sighed again. "I think he's a remarkable gentleman who cannot break free from the past and is in desperate need of love." She stepped closer and embraced her. "And you are just the woman to break the spell that holds him."

"Thank you, Evelina." She relished the hug from her sister. Since Alexandra had married, it was just the two of them. Oh, they still had Aunt Imogene, but it was different. Sisters shared a special bond. And then it struck her. "Is this what you meant by life changing?"

"I suppose it is."

Theodora lifted her head and looked at her sister, looked at her features and into her eyes. Evelina had their mother's same jade green eyes and determination. Their dear mama had been taken from them too soon.

"No matter where life takes us, you, Alexandra, and I will always be sisters, and we will always be here for one another, no matter the distance."

A sad smile crept across Evelina's face. "I hope you're right."

"All you have to do is ask, and we will be there." She kissed her sister's cheek. "We will always be there." Just then the clock began to chime, signaling that the afternoon was giving way to night. "We should ready for this evening."

And with a simple nod of her head, Evelina retreated into her room. Theodora had a nagging feeling that something else was bothering her sister but knew to give her time.

DINNER WAS THE same as the previous nights. Guests enjoyed an elegant display of culinary delights expertly prepared by Cook, the conversation was light, and laughter filled the dining hall. And Damian kept his distance, always watching, never joining. Although the mask he wore did not cover his mouth, he'd decided long ago not to partake in a meal with others, save his cousin and aunt. But he never removed his mask, never revealed the scars to anyone. Only in the privacy of his study, bedchamber, and his music room did he remove the cover, and even then, the mask was only an arm's length away. Shadow was the only other living being to see him without his mask and he intended to keep it that way.

Once dinner concluded, the guests retired to the parlor where card tables had been set up. After another lecture from his aunt, followed by nearly thirty minutes of pleading from Horatio, Damian rather reluctantly agreed to join the games this evening.

He paced outside the parlor several minutes before he sucked in his breath. *Let's get this over with.* As he entered the room, numerous sets of eyes settled on him. He wished he had Shadow next to him—just his presence was comforting. But Aunt Esther had informed him that a couple of the ladies were terrified of the large dog, though he happened to be the gentlest creature Damian had ever encountered. Thankfully, the stares did not last long, and the guests returned to their games, but his torture was just beginning.

An abundance of candles had been lit allowing for guests to see their cards, and worse, there was no dark corner for him to retreat to. His aunt had disobeyed the most important order he'd given.

What in bloody hell was he thinking, joining the others this evening?

It was one thing for him to host a country house party while keeping to the shadows, and quite another to entertain the guests. *Your guests.* He could feel the pull within his body. *Retreat . . . retreat.* But he didn't want to disappoint his aunt or cousin. He'd seen the hope in their eyes when they'd each requested that he join in the entertainments. After all the support Aunt Esther and Horatio had shown, he felt he owed them this.

As if sensing his thoughts were about her, Aunt Esther approached. "Thank you for joining us this evening," she said with a warm smile. He'd been rather harsh about all the planning for the house party and was thankful his aunt had stepped into the role of hostess. Bowing to some of her wishes was the least he could do. "I believe Lady Vernon's table needs a fourth player."

Damian followed his aunt to where Lady Vernon was seated. There were two other guests already seated—Miss Theodora and Lord Spalding. How was it possible that he was to be seated with the very woman whom he could not stopping thinking about, dreaming about? How was he to survive the evening?

"Lord Grimsby will be your fourth for whist," Aunt Esther announced, then turned to him and murmured for his ears only, "Behave yourself."

Damian always behaved himself. He'd never got into any real trouble as a child and had been a most dutiful son. He'd always taken his studies and responsibilities seriously, so what could his aunt be alluding to? So lost in his thoughts was he, that he hadn't realized the trio was waiting for him to sit until Lord Spalding cleared his throat.

Avoiding making eye contact with those at the table, he took his seat. He wasn't accustomed to being this close to others in broad candlelight. He was fighting the urge to dash out of the room to a dark corner of the house when a sweet voice coerced his attention. "Do you enjoy playing whist?" Theodora, who was on his left, asked.

Good manners had been drilled into him as a child. He could not ignore or refuse to make eye contact, and so with some reluctance, met her gaze. "Truth be told, it has been years since I've played," he admitted with some guilt. Over the last decade he'd kept to himself and only entertained Victor—before his untimely death that was—Horatio, and his aunt.

"It's been quite some time for me as well," she offered with a smile, putting him a little more at ease.

He was surprised by her response. She was vivacious and beautiful, and he assumed she would enjoy all such diversions and have many admirers. It may have been many years since he was in Society, but most ladies had enjoyed playing cards then. "I would have thought you enjoyed these sorts of activities."

"I much prefer musicales and playing the pianoforte." A slight giggle escaped her lips—her lovely, deep pink lips. "I always thought it would be a lark if I could have a pianoforte outside. I would play to my heart's content under the vast blue sky or in the silvery moonlight. There is something so magical about being drenched in moonlight."

In that moment, Damian wanted nothing more than to order the staff to haul the piano out onto the veranda that very moment and watch her play under the star-filled sky.

"I suppose it is a silly notion," she added with a shyness he found quite endearing.

"Not at all. The only negative I have ever discovered with the piano is that it does not travel well." From a very young age, Damian had shown great proficiency in the instrument. His parents had ensured that each of their estates had the best piano available for him to play on his visits. Except for the journey itself, he was never far from his beloved instrument.

Conversing with Theodora about music felt like the most natural thing in the world. Damian could not remember the last time he'd felt such at ease with another person. It was as if . . .

A loud clearing of the throat broke through Damian's thoughts. Once again, it was Lord Spalding, recapturing their attention. He'd been so lost in their conversation he hadn't noticed the look of annoyance on Lady Vernon and Lord Spalding's faces.

"Are you ready to begin this round, Miss Theodora, Lord Grimsby?" Lady Vernon said in an irritated tone, clearly not interested in discussing music.

Damian nodded his head in acquiescence while Theodora stifled a giggle, revealing a slight half-smile. Oh, what he wouldn't give to see her full beautiful smile once again.

Soon, the teams were determined and Lady Vernon, who was paired with Theodora, dealt. Damian, leading the first trick, placed a ten of hearts on the table. The other players followed suit, continuing the play with hearts. Before too long, Lord Spalding played a high trump, winning the trick.

All through the game, he felt the stares and uneasiness from those around him, except Theodora. The couple of times he dared glance her way, her eyes were soft, caring, understanding. Never once did he feel pity from her. Although her presence was calming, there was something about her that disrupted his senses and stirred hopes from long ago. He attempted to rein in those feelings and focus on the cards in his hands.

By the time all thirteen tricks were played, Damian was ready to retire to the quiet solitude of his music room. Although his team won, he suspected it had little to do with him, and more so with Lord Spalding's competitive nature. He'd heard the man was a proficient card player.

"Thank you for the game." He then stood and politely excused himself.

Damian glanced over to where his aunt was seated, silently bid her good evening with a nod of his head, then took his leave before she could protest at his early departure. He'd done his duty and now it was time to retreat.

Chapter Seven

Although Theodora was physically tired, her soul was restless, and she did not want to retire. She wanted to play the piano, to listen to Lord Grimsby play. But propriety dictated that she stay in her room, not wander in the night, for fear of stirring gossip or creating scandal.

But I'm not wandering. I have a destination in mind.

And besides, all she wanted to do was talk with Lord Grimsby and listen to his music. There certainly was no harm in that. With her mind made up, she grabbed her shawl and crept from her room, making her way through the house.

As she neared her destination, soft musical chords drifted down the hall. She was curious as to what he was playing. She had been studying music for as long as she could remember—her parents had not only encouraged her art, but indulged her, giving her scores of music to perfect. But she did not recognize the piece.

Lord Grimsby did not look her way when she entered the room but continued to play. She didn't say anything, simply wanting to enjoy the music. Theodora took a seat beside the fireplace, near to where Shadow was sleeping peacefully, and tucked her legs beneath her skirts.

Only when the soft chords came to an end, did he

acknowledge her presence. "Good evening, Theodora." Her name whispered past his lips, and it was music to her ears. Her heart skipped a beat, just as it had done the day of the treasure hunt. And in that moment, something changed between them.

"Good evening, Damian." She held her breath for a moment, hoping he would not turn her away. She suspected he was in need of a friend, in need of so much more. When he didn't respond, she added, "That was quite beautiful. Who is the composer?"

His shoulders sagged and his gaze lowered, staring at the keys that his hands were still resting upon. The two words came as a soft whisper, almost as if they were spoken in embarrassment or fear. "I am."

What stirred the imagination to be so creative?

"It truly was magnificent." He kept his head lowered as if unworthy of her praise. She thought to try a different tactic. "What was your inspiration?"

He looked over to where she sat. Although his mask hid part of his features, the struggle within him was palpable. How could she reach him, help him to understand? She wanted him to open up to her, to confide in her, to share a part of himself. Then once again, his gaze shifted back to the piano keys.

"Certainly, you must have felt some inspiration." It was more of a statement than a question. He did not answer. He didn't even move. If it weren't for the slight rise and fall of his chest, she would have thought him a statue. She was becoming almost desperate to reach him. Why couldn't he just talk with her? She suspected he wanted to but was afraid. She thought for a moment. Perhaps there was a less personal topic they could discuss. "Do you have a favorite composer?"

The lines on his face eased. He glanced over to where she sat, and with more confidence said, "Johann Sebastian Bach."

Theodora was very familiar with the works of Bach and counted them amongst her favorites. "Ah yes, there is a truth and beauty to his music that eases the soul."

And with her words, he began to play a beautifully moving melody by the master composer. Theodora closed her eyes and let the music consume her. There was a connection and intimacy that passed between her and Damian that was nothing like she'd ever felt or experienced.

"Thank you," she whispered, barely holding in the emotion.

"For what?"

"For playing for me." He was across the room, sitting at the piano, and yet the space felt intimate, like they were sharing something private. She supposed they were, and so she said as much. "For sharing a piece of you."

Silent seconds drew out before he finally murmured, the words struggling from his mouth, "You should go." And then he started to play another moving sonata.

She didn't want to leave, nor did she want to argue. She was at a crossroads. As she stood, the music drew her in. She drifted toward the piano as if not in her own body. She was unable to resist the intoxicating sound he created. It was as if he was begging her to stay through music.

And then slowly, the sound decrescendoed. She was standing only a couple of feet from the large instrument, but he had yet to glance her way.

"What do you want? What do you desire?" As the words brushed past her lips, she prayed he would answer.

WHAT DO YOU want? What do you desire?

It had been so long since someone had asked him, that Damian didn't know how to respond. What he truly wanted was an unattainable dream. He stared down at his hands, and the scar that ran across the top of his left hand, disappearing into his sleeve. The loneliness was pressing against his chest. He should order Theodora to leave, beg her to leave. He met her gaze and the words poured from his mouth. "Peace from the demons in my head."

"I know something about that."

She was young and intelligent, accomplished and beautiful, and should have no care in the world. "What could you possibly—"

"My father." Her gaze shifted off into the distance as if recalling a different time. The edge of her lips dipped into a frown; sadness filled her words. "Night after night, the demons tormented him, ripping away precious memories. And when the sun rose each morning, a little more of his spirit, his self, had been ripped from him, leaving him in a state of constant confusion. And all I could do was stand by his side and watch." She looked him directly in the eye, holding his gaze. "You are not the only one to have suffered, to continue to suffer."

He could feel her pain and desperation press against his heart. "Is that why you wander alone?"

"Yes. I miss him most terribly," she confessed. "I used to wander with him through the darkest of hours, trying to help him find peace. Trying to convince him—and perhaps myself, too—that all would be right." Tears glistened in her eyes as she worried her bottom lip. "I . . . I wish I could have done more for him."

"I understand that all too well." Emotion choked his words as he confessed. "I couldn't save my father or brother. I . . ." He closed his eyes, trying to shut out the past.

It was the most he'd ever shared of himself, of his innermost thoughts. Not even when he was engaged to Justine had he shared this much, and he'd certainly never played any of his compositions for her.

You are on dangerous ground. You're only going to hurt her. You must stop this. Now!

"Damian?" His name on her lips only acerbated the struggle, the turmoil within.

"I must retire." He stood and brushed past her, and when he did, he caught a whiff of vanilla. "Shadow, come." The dog eyed him with disdain. Clearly, he was content by the fire, but in the end, he followed Damian out of the room.

He'd only taken a few steps into the hall when he heard the first chords drift toward him, begging him to return. He didn't know how long he stood there, paralyzed in fear. Fear of taking a chance. Fear that he had revealed too much of himself. Fear that he was not good enough for her.

In the end, common sense dictated that he return to his chamber and forget Miss Theodora Grace. He would keep his distance, only attending events that were absolutely necessary. How he would achieve this monumental task, he was unsure. All he knew was that he must.

THEODORA WASN'T EXPECTING Damian to make an appearance at dinner, but she was disappointed that he did not join everyone after for cards and billiards. He had seemed to enjoy playing whist the previous night, but that was before they'd both talked about the past. Was he embarrassed that he'd revealed so much? He certainly should not be.

She enjoyed being near him, talking to him, listening to him play. She wondered if he ever played for anyone besides Shadow. She tucked those thoughts away for later, wanting to just enjoy the evening with her sister and friends. Something was bothering Evelina, and although she knew her sister would not discuss what it was, just being together helped.

While numerous guests gathered to play cards, Theodora, Evelina, and Miss Raine walked toward the billiard room, where some of the others had already gathered. The room, like the rest of the house, was most impressive with high ceilings, large windows, several billiard tables, and an abundance of space to play the game.

"Are you prepared to lose tonight?" Evelina teased as she picked up a stick.

"If I lose, it will be because you cheated," Theodora jabbed with sisterly affection.

"I wish I had a sister to playfully argue with," Miss Raine sighed. "My brother only knows how to argue the regular way."

Just then, Lord Raine's deep timbre flowed from behind. "Perhaps if my sister didn't always test the waters, I wouldn't have to argue so much."

"James!" Miss Raine turned and rushed into her brother's embrace. "You came! I didn't think you would, but you did!"

He glanced past his sister to Evelina, who was practically shooting daggers at him. What was it about Lord Raine that always had her sister on edge? And it wasn't as if Theodora could ask her sister—that only resulted in a tirade about said lord who was not to be mentioned by name. If she didn't know any better, she would have thought Evelina had formed a *tendre* for the rake, but her sister had vowed never to succumb to a rake's charm.

"Only for a couple of days. I am expected at our uncle's and thought to break my journey here to see how you were faring and what trouble you've stirred, little sprite." Although he spoke to his sister, his gaze kept traveling to where Evelina stood, arms crossed, and clearly annoyed.

Theodora could tell Evelina was beyond agitated by the arrival of Lord Raine and was only barely maintaining her composure. Her narrowed eyes, firm stance, and not-so-subtle huffs said it all. Ever since their time in London this past Season, Evelina had reacted thusly whenever Lord Raine was present or even mentioned. And when Theodora and Alexandra had previously questioned her about it, her only response was that he was an odious rake and not worthy of her attention. A distraction was very much needed before Evelina unleashed her fury.

"Shall we go find Aunt Imogene in the card room, Evelina?" Theodora suggested as she placed a gentle hand on her sister's arm, hoping to calm the rage that was simmering.

Her sister slammed the stick on the table, then whipped around and stormed toward the door, but not before casting a tempestuous eye at Lord Raine. Theodora offered a quick apologetic smile, then followed her sister.

"What was all that about?" she whispered as she rushed up to Evelina, who was already halfway to their destination.

Evelina threw up her hands and, in a whisper—a very forceful one—said, "Why does *that* man feel the need to attend every function I am at?"

Theodora tried to be the voice of reason. "It is only natural for him to attend. His sister is a guest here after all."

Her words fell on deaf ears as Evelina launched into a tirade. "Why does that unpleasant scoundrel have to be here, ruining the festivities? Oh, and he pretends he cares but . . . oh!" she huffed in exasperation. "Isn't it bad enough their aunt is in attendance and making everyone miserable?"

Miss Raine's aunt was without a doubt, one of the most unpleasant persons of their acquaintance. It was clear that she did not want to chaperone her niece and was only doing so to earn the favor of wealthier relatives. At every meal, at every event, she found something not to her liking. She wasn't overtly rude or impolite. She just expressed her constant displeasure in a way that seemed like a perfectly normal part of her personality. Nonetheless, it was very tiresome.

Just then, Lady Vernon and Lady Gordon strolled out of the card room, eyeing them both as if they were doing something untoward.

"Evelina," Theodora said as she grabbed her sister's hand and practically pulled her away from the two women. In a hushed tone, she added, "Later. Do not let him get the better of you."

Theodora pulled her sister toward the card room, where they joined their aunt and Lord Neave in a game of whist. Theodora was pleased that within a short amount of time, her sister had calmed and seemed to be enjoying herself. She hoped Evelina would confide in her later, but Theodora would not hold her breath. Evelina was reluctant to share much of what she was feeling lately, and Theodora didn't know what to do about it.

Perhaps they would be able to arrange a visit to see Alexandra. Perhaps their eldest sister could offer some sage advice. Aunt Imogene had told Theodora and Evelina to give Alexandra some time to adjust to married life, but surely enough time had passed. She would broach the subject with her aunt once the house party concluded.

"Oh, you won again," Aunt Imogene announced with great gusto. "That makes three wins just tonight, Lord Neave."

"And, as always, you are graceful in defeat, Lady Middleton," Lord Neave said in a charismatic tone. Was he trying to gain favor with their aunt in the hope of charming one of the sisters? They knew Lord Neave to be in want of a wife, but he'd never seemed interested in either sister. Since they'd started their salon at the beginning of the last Season, the sisters had all become very suspicious of gentlemen's ulterior motives.

Evelina's sharp gasp startled Theodora out of her musings. She was about to ask what had happened when her sister kicked her under the table, then slightly nodded in the direction of the doorway. She followed the direction her sister indicated and spied Lord Raine and Miss Raine strolling into the room as if they had not a care in the world. In truth, Miss Raine rarely did, but her brother . . . From the gossip that had circulated in London about him, Lord Raine had many cares, including paramours and scandals. Thankfully, Lord Raine did not stay, claiming that he was tired and wished to settle in for the evening.

"Thank the heavens," she heard Evelina murmur under her breath as she watched the rake leave.

Arm in arm, Miss Raine and Miss Ashton strolled toward their card table. "Good evening, Lady Middleton, Lord Neave, Miss Grace, and Miss Theodora. May we join your table?" Her words suggested that she was interested in more than playing cards.

Aunt Imogene must have picked up on that too, for she turned to Lord Neave and said, "Perhaps we should leave the young ladies to play. Would you join me for refreshments?"

"It would be my pleasure, Lady Middleton." He stood, then

offered his arm to their aunt, who glanced toward Evelina and Theodora and gave a sly wink. It was good to have an aunt who was an ally.

Miss Raine and Miss Ashton took the vacated seats, then glanced about as if assessing who might be noticing their true intentions. Without wasting time, the girls started a casual game, but none really paid too close attention to the cards at play.

"I didn't know how else to speak with you. Time is of the essence." The words rushed from Miss Raine's mouth. "My brother's arrival is such an unexpected surprise, but . . ." her words trailed as she glanced about the room, ensuring no one was listening to their conversation. Once satisfied, she continued in a hushed tone, "I fear that he may be opposed to a certain gentleman who has been most kind and sincere in his attention to me, and that I believe may be offering for my hand very soon."

Evelina leaned in and offered most emphatically, "If the gentleman is sincere and of good character, then you needn't worry. We will aid you." Theodora got the impression that her sister would take great pride in fooling Lord Raine.

"I was hoping you would say that," Miss Raine confessed, her features easing.

Miss Ashton nodded her head in complete agreement. "Of course, we all will. Friends aid each other."

And that was one of the reasons why the three Grace sisters had created their salon. While they pretended to play, the friends came up with ways they could divert Lord Raine's attention away from his sister. Of course, Evelina's was centered on tying the man up in the dungeon—not that they were aware of any such dungeon at Grimsby Hall. When Theodora said as much, Evelina amended her statement to having the rake thrown in prison and offering him only bread and water, which earned laughter from their two friends. Little did they know, Evelina was quite serious in her suggestion.

Theodora thought for a brief moment of asking them what she should do about Lord Grimsby, but she didn't think they would understand. He wasn't the typical gentleman a lady would form a *tendre* for, and yet she had. He was what she'd always hoped for in a mate. He was kind and sincere, passionate about music, and a good person. What she felt was too precious to share, at least at the moment.

First, she needed Damian to talk with her.

Chapter Eight

A UNT ESTHER HAD been none-too-pleased that Damian had not joined in for cards and billiards last evening. She had even gone so far as threatening to leave Grimsby Hall, leaving him to host the remaining week on his own. He knew it to be an empty threat, but just her stating it made him realize he needed to make a greater effort, if nothing else for her sake, despite his own reasons for wanting to avoid others.

At the very least, he would not have to play host this evening, though unfortunately, this evening's ball was one he must attend. When Lady Hamilton requested your presence, you did not deny her. No one, including Lord Hamilton, ever said no to the formidable lady. Over the years, Damian had become a master at avoiding Lady Hamilton during certain times of the year.

He glanced at the clock on the mantel in his study. The appointed time for their departure was approaching, and his aunt was certain to be anxious about leaving promptly. After giving Shadow some affection, he headed out.

The arrangements had been made for carriages to take his guests to Thynne Park—Lord and Lady Hamilton's extravagant home—making certain that he was traveling alone. He did not want to keep anyone's company this evening. He would watch the merriment from the corner and after an appropriate amount of time, would take his leave with none the wiser. Then he could begin tomorrow with a renewed effort to assist Aunt Esther.

"It promises to be a lovely evening," his aunt said as he stepped next to her. "I see the carriages are all assembled." He could feel her gaze upon him as she waved her hand toward his private carriage and spoke the next words. "Shall we depart?"

Aunt Esther could not possibly be implying that they were traveling together this evening. He'd given specific orders that he was to journey alone.

As if she could read his thoughts, his relative responded in a calm, orderly tone, as if what she proposed was perfectly acceptable. "Lady Middleton, Lady Vernon, and I will be in your carriage this evening. The other chaperones and gentlemen will have their own conveyance as well. The young ladies are quite excited at the prospect of journeying together."

He didn't want to keep company this evening. The whispers, the stares . . . These sorts of events were trying enough as it was. How much was he expected to endure in order to secure the earldom? He needed an excuse . . . quickly. "Isn't that inappropriate for the young ladies' chaperones to be—"

"Traveling in the carriage directly behind ours?" She shook her head. "I don't believe any scandal will arise. And if any of the ladies decide to bolt, they will certainly not get far in their evening attire," she ended with a tease.

Aunt Esther was testing his patience this evening.

With the guests in their designated carriages, they were soon on their way. Damian kept his gaze focused on the moonlit night. The full moon was bright and bathed the landscape in a silvery blanket, illuminating the road for their journey. Despite the beauty all around, anxiety coursed through his veins. He wished he were at home with Shadow, enjoying the quiet companionship with a good book by the fire.

THEODORA WAS PLEASED that Lady Stanbourne—with Aunt Imogene's influence, most likely, had arranged for her and Evelina to ride with their three friends to Thynne Park, while the other guests were divided among the other carriages. There had not been many opportunities for the friends to converse about their usual salon topics over the past week, and so this moment together, out of eyesight and earshot of nosy chaperones, was important. There were to be numerous gentlemen present this evening and they needed to expand their knowledge of the opposite sex.

"Remember, if you require assistance or a problem arises, use the code *By Zeus*," Evelina reminded them. "And never find yourself alone or cornered by a rake. That could lead to disastrous results. Any questions?"

"How do we capture a gentleman's attention?" Miss Ashton questioned with eagerness.

If Theodora knew the answer to that question, she would have certainly tried it on Damian. No matter what she tried, she could not break through the tribulations from his past. She rubbed her temples, trying to ease the ache from lack of sleep and too much thinking. She was at such a loss.

"I noticed that when men are interested in a lady, they gaze at her," Miss Raine began, "But we have been taught to be demure, and hide our interest behind a fan or deep blush. What if we try their technique? Hold their gaze until they blush." She stopped, then started to giggle. "Do men even blush?" She shook her head. "Regardless, I overheard my brother advise a younger cousin on how to be a rake, saying it definitely entices him."

Evelina sucked in her breath at the mention of Lord Raine. Although he'd said he was to attend this evening's ball, he'd not departed with them. In fact, there had been no sign of the rake all day. Theodora suspected her sister had had words with the not-so-gentlemanly gentleman, but Evelina was firm in her stance of not discussing said *non-gentleman*. Men were far too complicated to comprehend at times.

"That would be considered inappropriate and none of us can incite chatter or scandal," Miss O'Donnell practically scolded with a tsk. "We cannot compromise ourselves to gossips."

"But we're not in Town. The usual wagging tongues are miles and miles away. What better place to test this strategy?" Miss Raine argued.

"I think it worth a try," Miss Ashton agreed.

With a strategy settled, the girls chatted about who was on the guest list for the evening, who should be avoided, and what they were looking forward to most. With the full moon lighting the way, it was a pleasant journey. Theodora always enjoyed nights such as this—not the ball, but the moon in all its glory. She had always been fascinated by the many phases of the moon. Through the dark hours with her father, even when the moon was hidden, it was a constant companion, one she knew would always emerge to light the path.

They traveled along at a comfortable pace and a short time later they arrived at the grand home. The house had been beautifully decorated with swags of greenery draped across every surface and large topiaries guiding the guests to the magnificent ballroom.

"I certainly hope you-know-*who* will not make an appearance this evening," Evelina said behind her fan. The *who* in question was, of course, Lord Raine. Theodora still had not figured out why Evelina's emotions were so out of proportion against the lord. She knew that Evelina claimed she was certain that he did not care for poetry, he was a rake, and he had accused her of seducing him at Mrs. Fleming's dinner party this past Season in London. But other than a few brief encounters, the pair rarely saw each other. It mystified her why Evelina should continue to spend so much time fretting over him and his actions.

"Well, even if he *does* attend, you mustn't let him get the better of you. Just remember our code, and we will come to your aid," Theodora reassured her sister.

Evelina's features softened and her smile widened. "Thank

you. I'm sorry I've been so out of sorts lately. It's just that *he* frustrates me so much, I just want to—"

"Good evening, Miss Theodora, Miss Grace," Mr. Eastwick greeted as he approached. "Miss Theodora, would you do me the honor of the next dance?"

Theodora nodded in acceptance and took his offered arm. She would have to wait until later to discover what Evelina was about to reveal.

OVER THE YEARS, Lady Hamilton had invited Damian to her annual summer ball many times, but every year since the tragedy, he'd purposely stayed away from Grimsby Hall and this part of the country altogether, opting for one of his other estates. This year, however, he'd been unable to avoid the invitation. Securing the legacy of the earldom was becoming quite the strenuous task.

"Good evening, Lord Grimsby," Lady Hamilton greeted. She didn't stare at the mask he wore, or even look away, but met his gaze with warm affection, understanding even. Lord and Lady Hamilton had been good friends with his parents, and afterward, both had expressed concern for the family, always offering kindness and support. Lady Hamilton had been a constant friend to his mother and was even there the day she passed away. "I'm glad you finally have agreed to attend one of my balls. Now, go and enjoy the evening." She leaned in slightly, and said for his ears only, "And do not depart early, my lord."

He'd only just arrived and Lady Hamilton already suspected his intentions for the evening. Had his aunt confided in the longtime family friend and asked her to waylay him? He certainly would not put it past Aunt Esther to enlist everyone in attendance this evening to aid her in her cause. He would just have to be more artful in his escape.

Damian kept to the perimeter of the ballroom, attempting to

conceal himself the best he could despite his height. Anxiety started to roil within. There were no dark corners to withdraw to, no alcove to hide in.

He watched as the couples lined up for the next dance. And then the music began and he watched as the couples maneuvered through the lively dance, when all of a sudden, he spied Theodora dancing with Horatio, and his spirits sank even lower. They made a handsome pair.

What if Horatio chose Theodora for his bride?

The thought ripped through him, striking at his core. They seemed to suit well enough, and his cousin was an exceptional young man. Damian was certain Horatio could make Theodora happy. He knew he himself could not have a future with her, but he could ensure her happiness. Theodora would be the perfect countess for the earldom.

One thing was for certain, he would not survive watching them build a life together. The decision was clear in his head. Once Horatio offered for Theodora, he would retreat to one of his remote estates, helping his young cousin and his bride adjust to their new roles from a distance. Now all he had to do was wait for the inevitable—Horatio's decision to marry Theodora.

Damian could not bear to watch the dance any longer. This was one of the reasons he'd stayed away from society. He didn't want to feel, to hope. It would only lead to more heartache.

So desperate was he to flee, he did not notice those around him, and as he turned to take his leave, he bumped into Lady Dufferin. Her face twisted in shock before she schooled her features. "I . . . I apologize Lord Grimsby," was all she said before scurrying away. It was always thus.

Heat rose up his neck as the walls started to close in on him. Despite the hour being early and the inevitability of incurring his aunt's—and Lady Hamilton's—wrath, he must leave. He desperately needed a quiet place to calm the anxiety coursing through his body, but guests were still arriving and he could not exit the way he came in.

Glancing about, he noticed the open terrace doors. He moved through the ballroom toward the glorious night beyond as stares all around penetrated him. What felt like an hour later, he stepped onto the terrace, the fragrant evening air an instantly soothing balm. Although he would have preferred to leave completely, this would have to suffice for now. He moved farther from the house, into the shadows, feeling much more himself once concealed in darkness.

Soon his life would return to the quiet emptiness he deserved.

THE DANCE HAD ended, another had begun, and all Theodora wanted to do was to go to Damian's side. Even with his mask firmly in place, she could sense he was not at ease. Her heart ached for him and the loneliness he insisted upon because of his guilt. But she knew him to be a good, generous person. If only he could see past his tragedies.

Theodora moved through the quadrille, lost in thoughts of Damian. When at last the dance came to an end, not wanting to dance again, she made an excuse to her aunt and quickly began searching for Damian, but he was nowhere to be found.

"Looking for someone?" Evelina teased as she approached.

"I . . . umm . . ."

Evelina leaned in and whispered, "He's on the terrace. I'll make certain no one sees you."

Theodora needed no further encouragement. With her sister by her side, the pair strolled through the room toward the terrace making casual conversation. They stopped near one of the openings and waited for their opportunity, which came a few minutes later when the very elegant and very wealthy heiress, Lady Wilhelmina, entered the room to much admiration.

Now was her chance. With Evelina standing sentinel, Theodora slipped outside, avoiding notice.

It was such a glorious night with the full moon bathing the land in a wash of silvery luminescence. She saw Damian in the distance, moonlight illuminating his mask. Much like her, he was a creature of the night. And much like her, he would not want to be caged inside when the moon was calling.

It was highly inappropriate, but she didn't care. She wanted to be with him, share nights like this with him. "I thought I might find you here," Theodora said as she strolled toward where Damian stood at the far edge of the terrace.

As he turned to fully face her, his gaze met hers. She could see the anguish, the heartache, and years of sadness held deep within the depths of those blue orbs. He opened his mouth, presumably to scold her for her impropriety, but she would not hear it. Not tonight.

She held out her hand. "Dance with me."

Demons and propriety seemed to wrestle within, but he did not say a word as he accepted her hand. Even through their gloves, the moment their hands touched, something electric and unique coursed between them.

The sounds of night and the gentle breeze became a symphony as he led her through a waltz in their secluded part of the terrace. It was a beautifully seductive dance, and quite scandalous. It was a moment she never wanted to end. How could she convince him what was in her heart? How could she help him fight past the demons?

Slowly, softly, the dance slowed, and he gently swayed with her in his arms, moving to a rhythm known only to their hearts.

"What are you doing to me?" The whispered question brushed across her cheek.

"Showing you the possibilities." She inhaled, relishing in the scent of leather and man.

"Theodora . . . I . . . I can't." The words tore from his mouth in a shaky whisper as he stepped away from her, creating a distance that made her heart ache. "You deserve so much more."

"I only want—"

"By Zeus!" Evelina exclaimed in a loud voice, disrupting the moment. "What a pleasant evening for a stroll. The ballroom is quite stuffy."

Theodora turned to see who was coming, but when she turned back to Damian, he'd disappeared. She supposed she should be thankful. There could be no talk of scandal if she were caught alone. She sucked in her breath, stamped down feelings of disappointment, and joined her sister, who had stepped onto the terrace.

"Mrs. Raine is on the hunt," Evelina murmured as she took Theodora's hand and guided her back toward the opening. "You can tell me all the details of your dance later."

No sooner had they reentered the ballroom when Miss Raine rushed to them in a panic. "By Zeus," she whispered with force. "By Zeus." A moment later they saw the reason for her distress. *Lord Raine.*

"A word, Daisy." He held out his arm and waited for his sister to accept. For the first time Theodora could recall, Lord Raine did not glance Evelina's way.

Miss Raine shook her head slightly, clearly not wanting to discuss whatever had caused Lord Raine annoyance. His eyes narrowed on her, and in the next breath, she accepted her brother's arm and left their side.

"Oh, *that* man is so . . . so . . . impossible!" Evelina grumbled. "Why can't he just let his sister be?"

"Let's not let *that* man spoil our evening." And with that both sisters attempted to enjoy the festivities, but Theodora suspected neither of them did.

The evening progressed as one would expect. More dancing. More pleasantries. More of everything but Damian who had completely vanished from the ball, like a phantom in the night.

By the time they were returning to Grimsby Hall, it was nearly daybreak. The morning sun would soon begin to wake the land, but Theodora wanted nothing more than to find solace in a piano. Although the evening's entertainments had been pleasant, her encounter with Damian on the terrace had left her wanting more—more dancing, more music . . . more. Theodora longed to hear him play again. She'd never experienced such passion and emotion as when he played. She hoped he would still be in his music room, and that after her sister and aunt retired, she could sneak away.

"I was pleased to see Miss O'Donnell conversing with Lord Neave," Evelina said as she joined Theodora on the sofa in their private parlor.

"Yes, it would appear that they've formed a *tendre*." Lord Neave was a pleasant enough fellow, but Theodora found him lacking. However, she was pleased for them. There was another topic she wished to broach with her sister and now was as good as any time to bring up the man who was not supposed to be named. "I was surprised that Lord Raine attended." Evelina cast a harsh glare her way. "Yes, I know I'm not supposed to mention *his* name. What is it about *him* that you dislike so fiercely?"

Before her sister could answer, a soft knock sounded on the door.

"Who would be visiting us now?" Theodora went to the door, and when she opened it slightly, she was met with a giggle.

"It's me . . . Miss Raine . . . Daisy," she whispered.

Theodora opened the door wide. "Is anything the matter?"

"I need advice. May I come in?" she asked as she worried her hands.

The time after an event had always been a special time for the Grace sisters. It was when speaking of entertainments often gave way to sharing their innermost thoughts. But like everything in their lives as of late, things were changing.

"Of course," Evelina said. "We wouldn't dream of turning you away." Theodora could practically hear the relief in Evelina's voice that she wouldn't have to answer her questions about Lord Raine.

"Thank you. I get lonely with only Aunt Ruth for company." She leaned in and giggled. "She is not what one would consider good company."

Theodora quite agreed. The older woman wore a permanent scowl on her face. Even when she was saying something pleasant or agreeable, her features were in a downward slope.

"Has any gentleman caught your eye?" Daisy said as she looked to both sisters.

Theodora suspected the advice Daisy required had to do with a gentleman, but she was clearly not at ease to discuss it quite yet. However, her question wasn't one Theodora was about to answer. Her fondness for Damian was too personal, and so she kept silent. Even Evelina avoided the question. Theodora had her suspicions regarding who had caught her sister's eye.

Evelina must have guessed Daisy's unease in revealing her conundrum, too. Although her sister was a master of keeping her own feelings hidden, she was never one to let others do the same for long. She gave a sly half smile, then turned the question around onto Daisy. "A gentleman must have caught *your* eye. Is that why you seek advice?"

That was the only encouragement Daisy needed. "There is one." Her cheeks reddened as she continued to list the gentleman's attributes. "He is kind, and very handsome, and oh so sweet. And . . . I think he may feel the same, but . . ."

"But . . .?" Evelina drew out the word for a couple of seconds.

Her features sagged, and her words were heavy. "I do not believe my family would approve."

"He's not a fortune hunter or a rake?" Theodora questioned with concern. The gentler sex could never be too cautious. They would make certain none of their friends fell victim to either of those types of men.

"Oh no, nothing like that!" Daisy worried her lip, then whispered, "He's a third son of viscount. Not impoverished by any means, but also not the titled lord my mother believes I should show preference."

Why did everything in their world always seem to come down to rank, title, and status? A person's value should not be based on those things, but on what was in their hearts. Theodora was about to say as much when her sister interjected.

"As long as he is of good character, that's all that should matter. Who is it?"

"Mr. Douglas Malone," Daisy said with a dreamy sigh. Clearly the young woman was besotted. "And I think my brother may suspect. He was quite angry with me over my 'lack of propriety' as he put it."

"And what constituted your lack of propriety?" Evelina questioned, her features hardened against the unjust treatment her friend was receiving at the hands of Lord Raine.

"We shared one dance this evening and a glass of punch." She shook her head. "That was it! And my brother went on and on about how I smiled and giggled too much at the *young buck*."

Daisy *was* prone to giggles, but Theodora didn't see any harm in that and was about to say as much when Evelina began rambling. "Of all the insensitive things your brother could say to you! There is nothing wrong with being pleasant at social functions, not that *he* would know anything about that. All that matters is that Mr. Malone is sincere in his attentions."

"Oh, he is! Or . . . I mean . . . I believe he . . ." Daisy paused for several seconds, then in a most serious and determined tone, said, "No, I know he is, but we never seem to have a moment together without either my aunt or brother intruding."

"Do not fret. We will aid you," Evelina said with equal determination. Not for the first time, Theodora suspected her sister would take great joy in thwarting Lord Raine.

"Oh, thank you!" Daisy cheered as she clasped her hands together. "You have become such good friends. I just knew you would be sympathetic to my plight."

The girls chatted for a brief time before Daisy finally returned to her room. Although the hour was quite late, Theodora was not tired. Far from it.

"Are you retiring?" Evelina questioned, then answered her own question. "Just don't get caught." She then winked and left

Theodora to her own devices.

Holding a small candelabra, she strolled through the house with only one destination in mind. She suspected that before the fire, there had been many happy memories made here. She could sense it. The house, despite its grand size, felt like a home. She said a silent prayer, hoping to bring that happiness back into Damian's life.

DAMIAN HAD RESISTED the urge to go to his private music room for fear of encountering Theodora. She continued to plague his every breathing moment. After their dance earlier, he'd thought of nothing else but her and the way she felt against him.

But as the moon drifted across the night sky, morning neared, and remembrances of their waltz continued to consume his mind, he could no longer stay away. The intensity of that single dance stirred his creativity. His fingers ached to stroke the ivory keys, for the passion within to flow through them. And so, he found himself moving through the house like a phantom in the night, drifting toward the sound his heart desired.

And when he entered the music room, he was rewarded with the sight of her, sitting at his piano, her fingers gliding across the keys. Damian had never heard, or seen, anyone play with such passion as Theodora. But there was also a serenity to how she played that had him utterly captivated.

He was mesmerized by the movement of her hands and the sway of her body as she caressed the ivory keys with firm delicacy. He wanted to know how those hands would feel on him. He knew he shouldn't think about that, but in this moment, he would allow his mind to drift to what could never be, what he could not allow.

There was obvious attraction, but she only saw a fraction of him. His body was scarred. He did not think he could stand watching the look in her eyes turn from desire to fear. He *knew* he could not endure watching her scream in terror at the sight of his scars. But as the music swelled, in that moment, he believed almost anything was possible. He could almost convince himself that a life with Theodora was possible. That children could . . .

No. A child would be frightened by him, frightened to be held by him. His own little sister had not wanted to see him for the longest time, and when she'd finally worked up the courage, she'd cried. And then their mother died, the cries worsened, and he'd sent her to live with Aunt Esther.

But Theresa wanted to see you again, wanted to come home.

Would anything have been different? Damian did not believe he was strong enough to risk that heartache again. His mind had been made up.

But his heart begged for chance. *If you don't surrender, how will you know?* His mind and heart were constantly at war with each other. What was he to do?

When the music came to an end, Theodora looked over to where he was standing. "I was hoping you'd join me."

She moved away from the piano and went to a chair beside the fireplace and waited. She didn't say anything, but it was as if she expected him to join her. The silence lingered and he found himself taking a seat opposite her.

No sooner had he sat down than she asked, "Do you believe in eternal love? In finding your soulmate, your one true love?"

Theodora's question took him aback. It was something he used to believe in, but . . .

"No. I don't . . . No." Damian's response was weighed down with uncertainty, with the knowledge that he wanted to respond differently. He looked away, hoping to avoid the subject, but he knew Theodora would not be deterred so easily. And so he braced himself for the inevitable.

"I think you do," she challenged.

"Theodora—"

"No." She held her ground, her tone turning almost forceful.

"You will not dismiss me so easily. I can see you're at odds with the past and—"

"At odds?" His voice bellowed, ricocheting off the walls. "You know nothing of the past, of what I endured."

"Because you won't share!"

He stood up and stormed the length of the room, back and forth. How was he to explain to her that his life was not like others, that he could not offer strolls in the daylight, Seasons in Town, and hosting parties? How could he explain that he was scarred and broken?

"Why do you insist on going at life alone?"

"Because everything I touch dies or runs away!" he roared.

"That's not true. You have Shadow and your cousin and aunt and—"

"Every member of my immediate family." His argument was sounding weak even to his own ears. But he could not escape the past. He could not escape the pain of not being able to save his father and brother. What if something happened and he could not save her? He could not live with himself if he brought harm to her. "I should not have come."

And with that, he took his leave. In the span of a breath, his one place of refuge crumbled.

Chapter Nine

T HEODORA WAS AT her wit's end with Damian. Why was he being . . . such a *man*? He would not discuss his feelings, but she knew he was hurting. He would not discuss the past, but she knew he felt guilty. If he would only open up to her, confide in her, then perhaps she could help. They had a connection, she felt it, and she was certain he felt it, too. She needed advice and decided her aunt, with her years of experience with the *ton*, was just the person who might be able to aid her.

"Aunt Imogene?" she questioned as she knocked softly, then entered her aunt's room. Just like her own, it was spacious and well-appointed with a lovely pair of chintz chairs flanking the fireplace.

The spot between her aunt's brows crinkled with concern. "Is anything the matter, dearest?"

"I need advice."

Aunt Imogene waved her hand toward the chairs. "Tell me what's troubling you."

Theodora recounted everything that had happened with Damian, including the late-night music sessions. Her aunt was most understanding and thoughtful in her attention.

"Lord Grimsby has suffered much through the years, and he probably still feels guilty over the death of his father and brother.

Pain such as that does not diminish."

"I suspected as much, but it wasn't his fault that he couldn't save them," Theodora argued.

"I know that, and you know that, and I suspect Lord Grimsby does as well, but he has not accepted it." Aunt Imogene's words softened, and her eyes focused on Theodora. "I think he fears losing someone he cares about."

A glimmer of hope soared through her heart. "Do . . . do you truly believe he cares about me?"

Aunt Imogene reached across and squeezed her hand. "I do, dearest. I most certainly do."

She'd tried everything she could think of. "Then what am I to do?"

"Perhaps you should speak with Lady Stanbourne," Aunt Imogene suggested.

Lady Stanbourne.

"Yes, of course. Who better than his aunt?" Theodora stood and kissed her aunt's cheek. "Thank you."

"You're most welcome. And if anyone can help him heal, it is you." Aunt Imogene stood and went to her side. "You have the kindest heart of anyone I've ever known."

She wrapped her arms about her aunt. "Thank you. I love you, Aunt Imogene."

Her aunt pulled back, surprise lining her features, and Theodora wondered when the last time—if ever—she'd heard those words. She knew she and her sisters felt it, had shown it in their affection, but never said the words.

"It's nice to be loved." She gently patted Theodora's cheek. "I love you, my girl."

My girl. She adored that endearment. *It is definitely nice to be loved.*

Theodora took her leave and went in search of Lady Stanbourne. The butler informed her that she was in her private parlor responding to correspondences.

A soft hum drifted past the open parlor door. Not wanting to startle Lady Stanbourne, Theodora knocked and waited for a response.

"Come in," a pleasant voice said. Lady Stanbourne turned and with bright smile, greeted her. "Welcome, Miss Theodora."

The parlor was just like the rest of the house: bright and sunny and beautifully decorated. This was clearly a lady's space with the soft colors and delicate white doilies. Although formal in appearance, it felt quite cozy, the sort of room that was ideal for entertaining good friends.

Despite the welcoming words and relaxed atmosphere, Theodora was filled with uncertainty. Would Damian's aunt find her impertinent for wanting to discuss her nephew? She swallowed hard, then forced the words past her lips. "Good morning, Lady Stanbourne, I was wondering if you have a moment to discuss—"

"My nephew?" Her eyes were full of love and concern for Damian.

"Yes."

"I was rather hoping you'd visit me."

"You were?" Shock and surprise laced Theodora's words.

"Yes," Lady Stanbourne said with gentleness. "I believe I may be able to shed some light on the situation. Please, have a seat."

Theodora took a seat at the table, and kept her hands neatly folded in her lap. It wasn't something that happened often, but she was nervous. Not to talk to Lady Stanbourne—the lovely woman put her instantly at ease with her kind words—but to discuss her feelings. Admitting her *tendre* to her own sister and aunt was entirely different than declaring her affections to Lady Stanbourne. She had not even been able to confess her feelings to her closest friends.

"Where to begin," Lady Stanbourne said as she tapped a long delicate finger on the table several times. "Perhaps near the beginning. My brother and sister-in-law, although their marriage was advantageous, married for love. Love—to give and to receive love—was all they ever desired for their children. And when Damian was but twenty, he thought he fell in love."

"Thought?"

"Yes. Damian was always a romantic at heart. When he proposed to Miss Brunwin, we all thought he'd found true happiness." Lady Stanbourne shook her head. "But she was only interested in wealth and connections."

"My brother's wife is much the same," Theodora reflected with some sadness. The sisters missed their brother, but Rachel put a wedge between him and the rest of the family. "What happened to Miss Brunwin?"

Lady Stanbourne's words turned most somber. "The moment she saw what the fire had done to Damian's face, she cried off."

"That's horrible!" It was no wonder that Damian hid in the shadows. In his darkest hour, when he'd lost all hope, the woman he thought loved him had deserted him. "Have you seen his scars?"

"Not since it first happened. And although they were bad, with time, scars tend to fade." She shook her head. "I suspect the emotional scars run much deeper than the physical ones. You see, after the tragedy, my sister-in-law never recovered from the loss of her husband and eldest son. She was never the same. I think Damian feels guilty for surviving."

"What happened to his mother?"

"She died of a broken heart about a year after the fire. It wasn't too long after that Damian sent Theresa, his sister, to live with me. The poor thing was so young and frightened, not of Damian's scars as he believes, but of what had happened."

"How old was she?"

"Twelve," Lady Stanbourne said.

Twelve. Tears stung the corner of her eyes. "That's so young." Theodora and her sisters had been young when their mother first took ill, but they had still had their father and each other. Damian and his sister had lost so much in such a short time.

Lady Stanbourne eyed Theodora for several moments, almost assessing her. "I think *you* may be just the one to help him finally break free of the sorrow that binds him."

They spent the next hour talking about the past, what Damian had endured, and about his sister. Guilt and fear had caused Damian to push everyone away.

After their conversation, although Theodora understood more, she was even more downhearted than before. Night after night, they shared music and stories, but come daylight, he retreated into his shell and would not acknowledge her presence. One thing was for certain, she was still no closer to figuring out what to do or how to reach him.

With most of the men off on a ride on the estate, the women were left to their own devices, and she was thankful for some time alone with Evelina. She needed the companionship of her sister who knew her intimately. She just wanted to talk without censure.

Theodora and Evelina decided to take a stroll, which turned into a very long walk on an exceptionally pleasant afternoon. The weather was perfect, the sky was clear, and it seemed as if all of nature was basking in the joy of a beautiful summer day.

They'd been silent for most of the journey, but there was one question on the tip of Theodora's tongue. She let out a long breath and asked the question she'd been dreading. "Do you think I'm wrong in my affection for him?" She waited for her sister's response.

Evelina stopped and turned to her. "What does your heart say?"

Theodora didn't have to think about it for even a breath of a moment. "That he is a good man, and that I loved him from the first moment."

"There you have it." Evelina gave her an affectionate, sisterly hug. "Now all you have to do is convince him he is worthy."

Easier said than done. If only someone could offer advice on how to achieve that monumental task. *What if she played . . .* No, she'd already tried that. *A dance under the moon . . .* Done that, too. *What—*

The sounds of a dog whining broke through her thoughts.

"Do you hear that?" Theodora questioned as she turned her head this way and that, trying to determine the direction of the sound. "There it is again." This time the direction became clearer. She took off in a sprint, heading toward the sound.

"Theodora, wait!" Evelina called from behind. "Be careful!"

She jumped over a large branch and lost her footing for a moment but quickly regained it. She stopped, waiting for the sound again. A loud whine echoed from beyond the trees. Not knowing what to expect, this time she did proceed with caution.

"Oh no," she cried as she spied a dog trapped by a branch. If not for the whine and bark, she wouldn't have known what sort of creature she was looking at, the poor thing was so covered in caked-on mud. "Shh," she cooed as she approached.

"Theodora, perhaps this isn't the best idea," Evelina whispered as she approached.

"Nonsense, it's just a dog." She gently stretched her hand out, allowing the animal to sniff. "It's all right. I want to help you." With caution, she approached until she was next to the dog. With even more caution, she inspected the creature. Someone had tied a rope around the dog's neck, and it had snagged on a downed branch, but it was clear the animal had been roaming for quite some time. Its fur was matted and crusty with layers of mud.

"Is it friendly?" Evelina questioned from several feet away.

"Very." And if to prove Theodora correct, the dog licked her hand. She turned her attention to the rope. After several attempts it was free of the branch. "There you are. You're free to go." Theodora stood, then started toward her sister.

"It's following you," Evelina stated.

Theodora adored animals, especially dogs, as much as she did music. "Perhaps once we get to the road, it will be able to find its way home. Someone must certainly be missing this sweet creature."

As they continued on, every so often Theodora would glance behind and spy the dog following. Before long, the dog was at her side, smiling.

"It looks like were a party of three now," Evelina teased.

"Do you think Lord Grimsby will mind us bringing—"

"A very dirty dog into his house?" Evelina finished the thought. "Perhaps we should enlist the aid of one of the footmen and have the dog cleaned up before we broach the subject with his lordship—or Aunt Imogene for that matter."

Theodora hadn't even thought about whether her aunt would approve. "Do you think she'll mind?"

"No. Aunt Imogene has always been fond of dogs." Evelina's laughter echoed across the lush landscape. "Do you remember when she came to visit and Thalia managed to get into Aunt Imogene's traveling valise?"

"Oh, yes." Theodora laughed with remembrance. "She'd chewed her way through two pairs of Aunt Imogene's favorite shoes." Her dearest Thalia had been no more than a puppy of six months, and quite the mischief maker.

"Aunt Imogene took the mishap with good humor, even donating the shoe remains to Thalia." Evelina smiled as she shook her head. "I don't think she will mind at all. Now all we need is a plan."

Sometime later, the house was in sight, but Theodora and Evelina still had not formulated a plan, too distracted sharing memories from their childhood.

"We really do need a plan," Theodora said as she glanced at her new pup.

"Perhaps we should go to the stables instead?" Evelina suggested with uncertainty. "At least the dirt and mud won't bother anyone there."

It was as good a plan as any.

The sisters, along with their new four-legged friend, walked toward the stables. As they neared, a young lad greeted them and offered assistance. It seemed like it took days to cut away the matted fur and clean all the mud off the dog, but when they were finally done, she looked completely different.

"She looks so happy now," Theodora said as she petted the

dog's clean head. She was a lovely creature with a blonde coat and flecks of white all over. She reminded Theodora of a full moon, bright and drenching the land with light. "You are lovely, aren't you?" The dog smiled with her praise. "I think I shall call you Luna." The dog's long white tail waved enthusiastically.

"I think she likes her new name," Evelina said. "Now all I need to do is speak with Aunt Imogene about keeping her."

"And hope Lord Grimsby won't mind another dog in his house," Theodora added. "But until then, how are we going to get her in the house without anyone seeing her?"

AS IF DAMIAN didn't have enough plaguing his mind, he now had Aunt Esther intruding in areas beyond the normal house party duties, namely his personal life.

"Stop acting like a beast, Damian," Aunt Esther scolded. "You may have tried to fool the world, and perhaps yourself, but you have not fooled me. I know you better than that. And you have not fooled your staff or tenants. Your generosity is known and appreciated. You would see that if you looked beyond your damn mask!"

"Aunt Esther—"

"No. Do not *Aunt Esther* me." She put her hands to her hips as she began to scold him again. "I have tried to help you, but at every turn, you push me away. You push Horatio away. Why won't you let us help you?"

His patience was hanging by a thread. This conversation was becoming very tiresome. Why couldn't she understand? "Everyone judges by the way people look. Gossip and rumors always circulate about how handsome I used to be, how hideous part of my face is now, and—"

Her tone softened. "Is that why you keep your right side away from view? Because you think you're a monster?"

"Everyone thinks so," Damian stated the fact with certainty. He'd heard it too many times to count over the past years.

"Who? Theodora? She only wants to be part of your life, and at every step you turn away." Aunt Esther shook her head.

Theodora. She deserved better than a life with a scarred beast who was better suited to be a phantom than a man.

Damian was trying to forget her, forget what they couldn't have. "Why do you mention her?"

"I see the way you look at her," Aunt Esther said. "I may be a widow, but I remember what it is like to love, to feel love, to show love."

"It is none of your concern what—"

"You're wrong!" she declared with a stomp of her foot and a wave of her hand. "It is my concern. You are my nephew and my family. You are shutting people out and one day, you will find yourself truly alone. Alone and miserable and wishing for a second chance. Well, you've been handed a second chance now and all you can do is turn away."

Before he could defend his choices, Shadow's ears perked up, and then a moment later he was dashing out of the room with a yip and a bark.

Damian's words dripped with sarcasm. "As much as I would love to continue this conversation, I need to see what has disturbed my dog before he startles the guests again."

He and his aunt—who clearly was not done speaking with him—followed the sounds of Shadow's bark which echoed through the hall, sounding like more than one dog was in residence. Within a matter of minutes, they came to the source of all the commotion.

Theodora.

No, not just Theodora, but her sister as well, and a blonde and white dog who was playing with Shadow.

"What is going on here?" His voice rumbled through the grand hall.

Theodora did not shy away but held a firm chin. "Good afternoon, Lord Grimsby, Lady Stanbourne." She turned to the fair dog. "Settle down, Luna. You need to make a good first impression."

"Luna?" Damian and his aunt said in unison.

"Yes. We found her earlier with a rope about her that had snagged, but she was all muddy and dirty. We cleaned her up—"

"We?" Damian questioned, wondering who Theodora had enlisted to aid her. It seemed as if everyone was on her side, ready and willing to help.

The elder Miss Grace spoke first. "Yes, *we*. Theodora, myself, and one of your stable lads. He was most helpful in assisting with removing all the mud and grime."

Damian glanced heavenward. *Give me patience.*

"With your permission, of course, I would like to keep her in my room." It wasn't quite a question, asking for permission, but rather a statement that he couldn't refuse. And then Theodora smiled, and he knew he could not ignore her request. "She will be no bother at all."

Damian highly doubted that.

Chapter Ten

MUCH TO HIS aunt's continued displeasure, Damian had purposely missed whist and charades the night before *and* stayed away from his private music room. Despite the latter, the sweet intoxicating sound of Theodora playing the piano consumed his thoughts. He didn't know if she was truly playing and the sound wafted through the house, or if perhaps, he was just headed for Bedlam. But real or imagined, her music called to him, begged him to listen, not just to the music she played, but the words she spoke.

Aunt Esther and Theodora had given him too much food for thought.

By the time his mind had settled somewhat and he'd drifted off to a fitful sleep, the sun had already been bathing the land in light for a couple of hours. And it was much later by the time he emerged from his room.

Damian had missed the luncheon and lawn games. Not that he minded—he would rather be sequestered in his rooms with Shadow by his side—but he was certain to get another earful from his aunt later. As the day progressed, however, and he thought more about what his aunt had said, Damian admitted to himself that he wanted more, even if the more he could offer was only friendship.

"I thought I might find you here," Theodora said as she glided into his private music room as if it were not entirely improper for her to be here alone with him. Well, not entirely alone. Trailing behind her was the stray she'd found.

"I see you and your new friend have come to disturb me and Shadow." At the mention of his name, Shadow stood and went to Theodora and the other dog.

She leaned down to pet Shadow's head. "And how are you today?" she said as she rubbed him with enthusiasm. Much to Damian's surprise, her dog did not get jealous, but stepped in closer to Shadow and started to sniff him. "It would appear our dogs wish to be friends."

"Is that your ploy?" he teased.

"I need no ploy." She stood and faced him. "From the beginning, I have stated my intentions."

That she had. And yet something had changed between them. Or perhaps it was his aunt's admonitions still on his mind. Or perhaps he was opening himself up to Theodora's words. Regardless, he desperately wanted her to know him, to know his past. But was he strong enough to reveal that side of him?

So lost was he in his thoughts, he had not noticed that she was staring at him. But not in an uncomfortable, frightened way—the way most did when seeing him in the daylight with his mask.

His mask.

"Damian?"

"There is . . ." His chest rose and fell with each panicked breath. He closed his eyes, was this the right decision? Would it be revealing too much?

A gentle hand rested on his arm. "Damian . . . look at me." Her tone was tender, caring. He opened his eyes and met hers. "I want to understand. Please."

He inhaled deeply, then on a long, slow exhale, forced the words from his mouth. "There's something I want to show you." He took another jagged breath in. "That I need to show you."

She didn't back away, but simply waited for him to explain. He moved toward the paneled wall and pressed gently on the wainscotting. It clicked slightly open, but he didn't open it all the way.

"I'm certain you've heard . . ." The words lodged in his throat. Sharing this part of him was proving to be more difficult than he'd ever imagined. "After . . . that is, after I healed and could move about, I knew I would not be able to go about in the world as I once had." He wasn't prepared to share how those around him had reacted when they'd first laid eyes on his face. He didn't know if he would ever be strong enough to reveal that. "And . . . and so, I studied leatherworking. I learned from a tanner and leatherworker how to create . . ."

The words should not be this difficult to say. He was wearing a mask at that moment. Maybe he was wrong in trying to share this. It was deeply personal.

Theodora went to his side and once again, placed a gentle hand on his arm. "Show me."

What was it about this woman that gave him courage? Without further hesitation, he opened the panel, revealing a dozen half-masks hanging on the wall.

Theodora studied the numerous coverings. "Who made . . . ?" Her eyes met his. "You made all of these?" she asked as she waved her hand.

"Yes," he replied with some embarrassment.

Her hand tenderly brushed across one of the masks. "How?"

"For the longest time, I wore a silk mask that covered my entire head. As some of the wounds healed, I was desperate to feel normal, but no matter how hard I tried, I could not leave my room without a covering on my face. Harold—my butler— encouraged me to speak with his brother who is a leatherworker. He showed me how to cut and prepare the leather. Once I had a template that was comfortable for my face, I prepared the leather with moisture and heat until the form was set."

"They're each a work of art," she said with awe as she picked up one of the masks and inspected it. "Truly remarkable."

Her words touched his heart. "Thank you. I've had years to perfect it."

"Does anyone else know you created these?" she asked while inspecting another design.

"Only Howard. And now you."

He found her warm smile and sincere curiosity endearing. "Why do you keep them here?"

"This is my private space. No one"—*save you*, he refrained from adding—"ever dares to disturb me here. The masks are hidden away, locked up."

"*You* don't have to be hidden away or locked up." She reached up and cupped the side of his masked face. "Your scars are part of who you are. You tried to save your family. Almost died trying. But you've pushed away your sister and all who've loved you."

"How do you—"

"Your aunt," Theodora confessed as she worried her delectable bottom lip. "You kept your distance, and I was most . . ." She swallowed hard but didn't finish her sentence. "She loves you dearly. She wants you to be happy, to have a full life."

Sounds of laughter drifted in from somewhere in the house. Damian took the mask from Theodora's hand and returned it to its place, then closed the panel, resting his head against the wood. "The guests have returned. You should ready for this evening."

Theodora did not object, didn't even say a word. She simply took her leave, with Luna and Shadow on her heels, leaving him alone with his thoughts.

Hours later, the guests had assembled and were enjoying themselves in the dining hall. Damian still was not ready to join everyone for a meal, but once the men rejoined the ladies, he decided he would as well. For reasons he could not explain, he did not want to be alone, but that did not mean he would sit near the others.

Keeping to a quiet, far too bright corner, Damian took a seat and waited for the entertainments. A moment later, Lady Middleton came and sat beside him. "My niece has offered to play for us this evening. She is a great lover of music."

Theodora situated herself at the large instrument. The moment her fingers caressed the ivory keys, his body calmed. He could not help but wonder if she had offered to play because she knew it would ease him, comfort him, make him feel part of the world.

Damian could not remember the last time he'd enjoyed an evening in the presence of others. And he had Theodora to thank for that.

ONCE EVERYONE HAD retired, Damian retreated to his private music room, certain that Theodora would come. It seemed destined to become a nightly routine for them and one which he was beginning to truly look forward to.

He played his favorite sonata and waited. He was only part way through when Theodora entered the room, sans Luna.

"Where's your dog?"

"With my sister." She moved to where he was seated at the piano. "I didn't have the opportunity to thank you for showing me your masks."

"You're welcome." For reasons he couldn't explain, he was nervous. Would she ask more questions of him?

"May I see your face?"

This was one question he wasn't ready to answer.

He started to argue, "You can see—"

"No. Without the mask." She held his gaze, her eyes begging him to acquiesce.

He didn't even look at himself without the mask, not even *with* a mask. The last time he'd gazed upon his reflection in a mirror was the morning before his world had changed into a fiery hell. The recoil from others had told him all he needed to know about his appearance. Perhaps if she saw the scars, then she would finally acknowledge the inevitable and leave him be. Leave him to a miserable existence. Alone.

But he didn't want to be alone. Not anymore.

I don't want to be alone, but what if she cannot stand the sight of me? There were too many conflicting emotions roiling through his body.

"Trust me," she whispered.

He closed his eyes and sucked in a deep breath. They were so close. He was paralyzed in fear, unable to speak or move.

Her hands moved across his face as she slowly, tenderly, removed the mask. Coolness caressed where the mask had just been. Damian waited for her to say something. She didn't gasp or make a sound.

Keeping his eyes closed, he slowly released his breath, but the tension knotting his insides remained. At any moment she would cry, declaring him a beast, and then he could return to his life of solitude, of guilt.

A softness brushed across his unscarred cheek and he realized it was her lips. Her gentle breath caressed his cheek, sending a warmth and desire he hadn't felt in such a long time. His hands ached to touch her flesh, to feel her softness. He opened his eyes but dared not look at her. She was a breath away, too close and yet too far away.

"What are you doing to me?"

"WHAT ARE YOU doing to me?" His whispered question brushed across her cheek.

It wasn't the first time he'd asked such a question, but she desperately wanted it to be the last. She wanted him to have faith in the love she offered, to let go of the past, and believe in their future. Long seconds passed before she spoke the words from her heart. "Loving you. I want to be your moonlight, filling the dark recesses of your soul."

"Theodora . . . you must go." Even as he said the words, he kept his hands firmly on her hips, holding her in place.

"Look at me," she begged firmly, then softened her tone. "Look at me."

He shifted his gaze and looked into her eyes. "Theodora—"

She didn't let him finish his protest, but brushed her lips to his, silencing him.

Theodora knew she was being far too improper, but she didn't care. She hadn't been afraid of what she might see, of the scars he'd tried to scare her away with. No. She was afraid of not seeing him ever again, of not experiencing this moment with him.

When she'd lifted the mask away from the right side of his face and stared into his clear blue eyes, she saw pain and uncertainty, but she also saw . . . goodness. He was a good man in desperate in need of healing and love. Her love.

When the kiss slowed, she eased back. Her eyes drifted from his eyes, studying his face. Two fierce scars slashed across his left cheek, contorting the skin. She suspected that at one time, the area had been red and sensitive, but now only flesh-toned ridges remained. She reached out and gently ran a finger down the smaller of the two.

He flinched but did not pull away.

"Does it hurt?"

He shook his head and whispered, "No."

Theodora then moved her finger to the larger scar, the one that traveled down his neck, disappearing into his shirt.

"How far does . . ." Her words trailed as her finger intimately caressed its way down to where skin and fabric met.

Damian grabbed her hand. His chest rose and fell as he spoke. "You shouldn't be touching me like this." His words said one thing, but the desire in his eyes said he was just as affected as she by the touch.

And Theodora was never one to back down. "Why won't

you let me—"

"Please Theodora, I am not strong enough."

With her other hand, she cupped his cheek and raised her lips to a breath away from his. "Not strong enough for what?"

"You need to return to your room."

"Why?" She was tired of him telling her what to do, when all she wanted was to be with him.

"Don't you understand?" He caressed her cheek with a tender finger. "I can't . . ." He struggled with his words. "Theodora, please go."

The pain that had been consuming him for years formed a wall between them. She didn't want to leave. She wasn't going to leave. She would not lose him. She knew he cared but could not get past the scars, which she did not care about. He was all things to her and . . . she was in love with him.

"No. I don't want to leave. I know you're hurting—"

"Theodora—"

"No. I will not leave. I love you, dammit!" She forced his shocked gaze to meet hers. She hoped her words were firm enough despite the emotion and turmoil coursing through. "I. Am. Not. Leaving." And to prove her point, she brushed soft kisses across his lips. "I am not leaving," she whispered softly.

"Why do you insist on unraveling me?"

"Because I'm in love with you." She didn't expect him to say it in return, but *she* had to say it. She had to let him know. Perhaps if she kept saying it, he would listen.

"How could you possibly be? It's not possible."

"Why is it not possible? Help me to understand."

"I . . ." As he closed his eyes, she could sense the struggle within him. He sucked in a deep breath, then said, "It's getting late."

Theodora eased back. She would not press—not yet at least—but she was not giving up. "Thank you for letting me see you." She brushed a kiss to his scarred cheek, then took her leave.

This was far from over.

DAMIAN SAT AT the piano, unable to play, to move. Had he just imagined Theodora removing his mask, tenderly caressing his scars, kissing him, declaring her love for him?

How was it possible that someone like her could love him?

Perhaps he'd just imagined that she was here, and those kisses were nothing more than phantom kisses. He was meant to walk this life alone. He didn't deserve to live, to have love and happiness while his brother was denied that chance.

Aunt Esther's words pushed to the forefront of his thoughts. *You've been handed a second chance and all you can do is turn away.*

Damian grasped his head in agony as conflicting emotions vied for his attention. He'd already lost so much and didn't know if he had the courage to risk his heart. What if something happened to Theodora? What if he couldn't save her? What if . . .

He must put an end to this once and for all.

Chapter Eleven

T HEODORA LAID IN bed, thinking about the kiss she'd shared with Damian, his soft lips on hers and the hunger in his eyes. She sensed his struggle, but she didn't know how to convince him to let go of the past, to trust the future. She threw back the covers and went to the window. Her words consistently fell on deaf ears. She was desperate to understand.

"How can I . . ."

The hunting lodge.

Perhaps if she saw where his life had changed so drastically, then she could understand. Lady Stanbourne had informed her that after the lodge had been torn down, he forbade anyone from going there.

Theodora was certain the answers she sought could be uncovered by starting at the beginning. She quickly dressed and grabbed her father's coat, then a soft whine caught her attention.

"Shh, it's all right girl. Stay here." She stroked Luna's soft head. "I'll be back soon."

Theodora crept through the house like a thief in the night, except that it was early morning. Perhaps she *was* a thief in a way. She wanted to steal the painful memories of Damian's past and lock them away where they could never torment him again. She thought if she could see the ruins, perhaps she would somehow understand his reluctance to let her in.

Thankfully, none of the servants took note of her as she snuck past them. Or more likely, her reputation for taking early morning walks aided in the diversion.

Pulling the edges of her father's coat more tightly about her, she stepped into the cool morning haze and headed toward the stables. Although she preferred to walk, Lady Stanbourne informed her that it was nearly a half an hour's journey on horseback, and that was with keeping a good clip. Even though Evelina had promised to make excuses for her, she could not risk being missed and certainly did not want to attract attention over her morning escapade.

With her mode of transportation decided, she headed toward the stables, and before long, she was on her way. Lady Stanbourne had also mentioned the location of the lodge when they talked the other day. It was as if she expected Theodora to investigate the site. She was thankful for the older woman's guidance and willingness to aid.

As she crested the slight hill, she saw the charred ruins of what once had been the hunting lodge in the near distance. Hot tears stung the corners of her eyes as a heavy weight of grief pressed upon her chest.

She brought her horse to a nearby tree and secured her while she went to explore. As she walked around and through the ruins, the ghosts of the past enveloped her. She could practically hear the cries and chaos, wood burning and debris falling. Damian had saved several people that day but had condemned himself to a life of sorrow for those he couldn't.

Theodora brushed her hand across a cold stone ruin and said a silent prayer. *Help me to understand.*

DAMIAN HAD TOSSED and turned through the inky night hours, his mind and heart again at odds with each other. No matter how hard he tried, he was unable to get Theodora out of his mind. What was he going to do about her?

He went to the window and gazed across the peaceful morning landscape when a figure in the distance walking in the direction of the stables caught his attention. *Theodora.* He would know her anywhere. She certainly had a knack for skirting society's rules. What was she up to?

Go to her, his heart begged.

What if something happened and he couldn't protect her? his mind reasoned.

Regardless, she shouldn't be out on her own.

With his mind somewhat made up, he decided he would follow her—not go to her, just to follow. He would protect her from a distance.

He quickly changed, and with Shadow following close, headed in the direction he'd last spied her, but as he neared the stables and there was no sight of her, dread filled him.

"Have you seen Miss Theodora?" he called to one of the lads.

"She went for a ride," the stableboy began, then his tone turned nervous. "I wanted to accompany her, but she insisted on going alone."

Damn. Anger and annoyance collided. He would not take it out on the lad. Theodora was too headstrong for her own good. "Saddle my horse, and have one of the other lads take Shadow back up to the house."

A short time later, Damian was headed in the direction the stableboy had indicated Theodora had gone. As the minutes ticked by, recognition of the surrounding landscape became clearer and demons from the past clasped a fiery claw about his heart.

She wouldn't dare go there. The thought thundered through his head. But as he crested the hill, he saw Theodora in the distance amongst the ruins.

Rage and hurt and sorrow and grief collided within, suffocating his entire being. He had to get away. He could not bear to be here as images and cries from the past flashed before him. *Hot embers raining down, swirling through the screams and chaos.* He turned his horse and kicked it into a gallop. *Damian, save me!* He had to get away. *John!* Now!

By the time he reached the house, the fury and turmoil within was at a boiling point. It took all his effort not to lash out at those he encountered as he stormed to his private music room, and slammed the door closed, rattling the walls.

Even once he was sitting at the piano, pouring all his anger and frustration into his music, there was no relief from the past, from the sorrows that tortured him, and the one woman who insisted on opening Pandora's box.

He didn't have to look up to know when Theodora entered the room and shut the door. He felt her presence even before her voice rose above the tormented chords he was playing. "I wish to speak with you," she said with the force of a lion.

All common sense snapped, and his fury unleashed. He pushed away from the large instrument. "What the bloody hell do you think you were doing?"

Her deep blue eyes were wide with shock, but she did not say a word.

"You went to the . . ." He ran a frustrated hand through his hair as he tried to force the words from his mouth. He swallowed hard. "You went to the hunting lodge. Damn it! Why did you have to go there?"

"To try to understand!" She started toward him, but he put up his hand to stop her.

"Why do you continue to plague me?" he grumbled.

"Why do *you* continue to shut me out?" Theodora held her ground.

He ran a trembling hand through his hair. The angry words poured from his mouth, reverberating around them. "Because I don't want you here. I don't want your friendship. And I certainly do not—"

"I understand," she said in an eerily calm voice. "You don't want to let go of the past. You would rather rot in misery than accept that someone may care for you." She shook her head. "I finally understand."

She turned and went to the door. She opened it and stopped in the threshold but did not turn to face him. "Goodbye, Lord Grimsby." She then stormed away, leaving him utterly alone.

Pain the like of which he had never felt slashed through his heart.

"Oh Shadow, what have I done?"

The dog did not answer, but seemed concerned about Theodora. And the next thing Damian knew, he was chasing after her.

WHAT JUST HAPPENED?

Theodora had done the one thing she'd vowed not to do. She left him. Nothing she said or done had got through to him. She didn't know what to think anymore. The pressure in her heart was pounding against her chest.

Dashing toward the stairs, she practically collided with Lady Gordon. "Is anything the matter Miss Theodora?" she said as she took several steps back in panic.

It was only then that she realized Shadow had followed her.

"Not at all," she lied with a pasted-on smile, as she rubbed the dog's large head. "Shadow and I are merely going for a walk." The woman continued to back away, giving Theodora and the dog a wide space to pass.

No sooner had she entered her room with Shadow—who seemed reluctant to leave her—than Evelina entered, followed by Luna. And a moment later, Aunt Imogene.

"Luna started whining, so I figured you returned." Evelina turned her gaze to where the two dogs were now lounging near the window, sunlight warming them. "Perhaps it was Shadow she was whining for," she said with a chuckle.

"At least Shadow isn't being difficult." *Unlike his master,* she thought.

"Come and sit," Aunt Imogene said. "Tell us what happened."

Theodora recounted the morning and her argument with Damian. No matter how hard she tried, no matter what she said, he wouldn't let her in, wouldn't trust her. *But he had revealed his scars to you.* Damian was such a conundrum!

"Why can't he see that his scars don't affect my opinion of him, that it is *him* I care about?"

Aunt Imogene took Theodora's hand in hers. "Be patient. He's spent the last twelve years building a wall, trying to protect his heart. I wish I had other words to offer, but he just needs time."

How much time? The house party was soon coming to a close and they'd be returning to Aunt Imogene's home. Theodora feared that if she left Grimsby Hall, she would never see Damian again.

Evelina embraced her. "It will all work out in the end."

Patience and time. Theodora wished she shared her aunt's and sister's sentiments.

THEODORA HAD NOT wanted to join in croquet, but she also didn't want to fester in her room, succumbing to the gloom. Even so, a distraction was very much needed, she thought as she aimed her mallet. A moment later, it was delivered.

"I have exciting news," Miss Raine whispered as she ran up to Theodora and Evelina. "And I need your help."

A moment later, Mrs. Raine—Daisy's aunt—trudged toward them. "I'm going to retire. I'm feeling rather tired." The older woman slowly walked past the curious guests, airing her grievances to no one in particular along the way.

When the woman was out of earshot, Miss Raine said, "My aunt has been complaining about all the sunshine and outdoor activities, but I think it is a glorious day."

Despite the morning encounter with Damian, it was a beautiful day. *Don't think about him. Patience, remember?*

"You mentioned something about needing our help?" Theodora said.

Miss Raine glanced this way and that, then said rather loudly, "Oh look, my ball is over there." The sisters followed their friend away from any curious onlookers. "Mr. Malone has proposed, and I've accepted."

"That's wonderful news! Does your brother know?" Evelina questioned. Much to Evelina's delight, Lord Raine had departed shortly after Lady Hamilton's ball.

"No, and that is why I need your assistance. Before he departed, he gave our aunt strict instructions about who was and was not acceptable for me to dance with. And marriage is much worse than a dance! He mustn't discover until after we elope. Please say you'll help."

"And when—"

"Tonight," Miss Raine said under her breath as she continued to glance about nervously for any eavesdroppers. "After dinner."

Evelina clasped her hands together, and with much enthusiasm said, "That doesn't give us much time to plan. Let's get to work."

The girls spent the remainder of the game, not quite playing, and most definitely scheming. Although aiding Miss Raine was providing the much necessary distraction, Theodora could not escape all the emotions churning within. She had not seen Damian or Shadow throughout the day and when she inquired after him, Lady Stanbourne said her nephew had gone off on estate business.

Theodora hoped that he would return before the house party was over. She didn't want to contemplate what it meant if he did not.

BY THE TIME the sun had set and the evening festivities were to begin, Theodora *still* had not seen Damian. Thankfully, aiding Miss Raine with her elopement plans provided an excellent distraction, which continued well into the evening.

"Everything is all set," Evelina said. "There are still a few days left of the house party and since your aunt is unwell and keeping to her bed, hopefully she will not notice you haven't gone to visit her."

"I highly doubt she notices anything. Aunt Ruth is just like my mother, only interested in herself," Miss Raine admitted with a frown.

Theodora felt for their friend. She was such a nice person to have relatives such as those. Especially a mother whose only cares revolved around her place in Society. Hopefully this new life would be what Daisy had always dreamt about.

"Remember the plan," Theodora reminded their friend. There were several crucial elements that would ensure success.

"When the ladies gather for cards, I claim a megrim and retire to my room," Miss Raine reiterated what they'd come up with earlier. "And I inform my lady's maid that I require darkness and quiet and should not be disturbed."

"Yes. Before we retire, we will say that we will check on you. I will send word to your aunt that you have a megrim." Evelina was the mastermind behind the plan, leaving no detail to chance. "In the morning, we will use the same excuse and send word to your aunt that you are still indisposed but improving."

She worried her hands as she spoke, "What if my aunt suspects?"

"Never fear, I'm certain Aunt Imogene will aid in our subterfuge if needed, but hopefully, we will not have to employ her. The fewer who know what is truly happening, the better." Evelina had thought of every last detail, even anticipating the return of Lord Raine. Although she had not revealed to Theodora how she would deal with that situation, she had assured her that she knew what to do and how to handle said lord.

"Since Mr. Malone has been staying with a friend nearby and has not been attending all the functions, his absence should also go unnoticed," Theodora reassured her friend. "Is your small valise packed?"

"Yes." A wide smile warmed Miss Raine's features. She was clearly in love with her intended.

"I think that's everything," Evelina said as she clasped her hands together. Her elder sister truly enjoyed aiding ladies to find their happiness. Now if only the two sisters could find theirs.

"Thank you both for all you've done," Miss Raine said she stepped in and drew them both into an embrace. "And for the kindness you've shown."

The evening came and went without issue. Miss Raine's performance was flawless, and no one questioned it when she claimed a sudden megrim. Mrs. Raine's continued illness, however, was noted briefly, but it was quickly dismissed by one of the elder women present who claimed that her friend always had some ailment. And then there was Damian's absence, which no one commented on. To those present, it was as if nothing was untoward. Only there was. The latter was causing Theodora much distress. She missed Damian's friendship.

The next day offered more of the same. Every detail was perfect, the food exquisite, but the company was lacking. Theodora desperately wanted to see Damian, to make amends, but her aunt, once again, told her to have patience and let him come to her.

Aunt Imogene, Evelina, Miss Ashton, and a couple of the other ladies ventured into the village, leaving Theodora wandering through the garden, alone with her too many thoughts. Well, not quite alone. Luna had become a constant companion. Plus, there were several guests enjoying a game of lawn bowling, but none seemed to take notice of her.

Inhaling deeply, Theodora relished the summer scents that reminded her of bygone days with her family, climbing trees, going for long walks, and just being together. They truly had always enjoyed each other's company.

Since her brief time in society, Theodora had learned that most families of the *ton* were not like hers. Quite the opposite in fact. She could not remember a time when her parents fought or argued or didn't want their children present. And except when her parents entertained, they'd always taken their meals together. Theirs was a most loving family, and one that she hoped and desired to emulate with her own future husband.

Husband.

Damian was the sort of man she'd always dreamt about marrying. Why did he constantly push her away? Did he not realize the scars didn't scare her? He seemed attracted to her, and she was to him, so that must not be the issue. Was it just the past or something more? If only he would share.

"I was hoping to find you alone, Miss Theodora." Mr. Eastwick's soft voice interrupted her ponderings. Perhaps he could enlighten her about his cousin.

"Good afternoon, Mr. Eastwick," she said.

She was just formulating her question when he blurted, "Could you help me?" His tone was most dire, and his features were strained, but he didn't look like he'd been physically harmed.

"Of course," she said as she waved her hand toward a large shade tree. Private enough, but still in view of the guests. The last thing she needed was a scandal or a forced marriage.

He shifted his weight from foot to foot, clearly not at ease. Beads of sweat started to form on the sides of his temples. "I . . . I was wondering . . . that is . . ." His face reddened as his breathing increased. What was so serious that caused him to be so troubled?

She had no clue why he was in his current status. Had something happened with Damian? Had he come to deliver unfortunate news? Concern edged its way up her body, settling into her heart. "We're friends," she began in a gentle tone. "Please speak whatever is on your mind."

The confession flew from his mouth at a rapid pace. "I'm in love with Miss Ashton but I get nervous when I'm around her and I desperately want to spend time with her but I don't know what to do or say without sounding like a bumbling idiot." He inhaled deeply and then slowly released his breath and added, "Much like I'm doing currently."

"That's excellent news!" she said, then quickly explained, "Not about you rambling, but the part about Miss Ashton." The anxiety she had experienced a moment ago dissipated, replaced by warmth and satisfaction. "Claudia is a wonderful lady."

"Do . . . do you think she . . . that is . . ."

Trying to reassure him, she offered a smile. "I think she does." She'd suspected her friend had formed a *tendre* for Mr. Eastwick, but she'd been guarded about revealing it. It was quite frustrating—for both parties, she presumed—to constantly wonder if the other's affections were the same.

"I don't know how to proceed. It seems as if there is never a quiet moment, and I . . . I just don't know what to do."

Without thought, Theodora reached out and patted his arm with reassurance. "Do not worry, Mr. Eastwick. I will assist you. And I am certain my sister will as well."

He placed a hand on top of hers. His breathing had evened, yet his voice still quavered with nervousness. "Thank you, Miss Theodora. I will be forever indebted to you."

EVER SINCE THEODORA had walked out of his music room, Damian had been in a foul mood. He did not want to contemplate the reasons why, either. Aunt Esther had stormed into his study a short time ago and tried to reason with him, but he had *his* reasons. And to make matters worse, his cousin had been skirting earldom responsibilities. Damian suspected the lad was rebelling over what was to be his future. He didn't want to leave his study and search him out, but when Horatio did not arrive at the designated time for the third day in a row, he had no choice.

Pushing away from his desk, he decided to search out Horatio. His need to instruct his cousin on running the estate outweighed his desire to avoid people. "Come on, Shadow."

With Shadow on heels, the pair stepped out onto to the veranda, but no sooner had the gentle summer breeze whisked past them, than Shadow ran off, exploring something in the distance that had caught his attention.

"Predictable," Damian chuckled as he watched Shadow investigate his findings. Damian stood on the veranda, admiring the view while searching for his cousin. Some of the guests had assembled outside to play lawn bowling, enjoying the bright summer day, but he didn't find Horatio amongst them.

It was too pleasant a day to stay sequestered in the shade, and so he decided to take a stroll in the direction of the garden, away from where the guests had congregated, and look for his cousin there.

As he neared, he spied a couple conversing. He squinted against the rays of sunlight as Horatio standing in the garden with Theodora came into focus. No, not just standing. Horatio appeared to be in deep conversation with her. And, worse still, his hand was atop hers.

Damian's heart plummeted, crashing into the depths of his empty soul. Had Horatio decided upon Theodora for his countess? Was she interested in him? But Theodora had shared a kiss with *him*. *And then you turned her away.* He took several steps to the side, concealing himself behind a large tree, and watched the exchange.

Pain ripped through his heart. This was exactly what he'd been trying to avoid. He didn't want to feel. He didn't want to want her. He'd tried to push her away, and this was what he got—excruciating turmoil rippling through him. Well . . . no more.

Turning on his heels, he stormed back into the house. He was done with feeling.

Chapter Twelve

Agonizing hours had passed since Damian witnessed the intimate interaction between Theodora and his cousin. He knew the time was quickly approaching when Horatio would come to him, revealing his choice of bride. Damian did not know how he would endure the heartache. If earlier was any indication, he would not endure it well. He wanted his cousin to be happy, but it meant him being absolutely brokenhearted in the process.

You did this to yourself.

He ran a shaky hand through his hair, gripping the ends as he went to his only relief, his piano. But before he could even sit down, the peace he sought was disturbed.

"Good evening, cousin," Horatio said in a cheerful tone as he entered the music room.

Damian glanced at the clock on the mantle. It was nearing midnight. *The time had come.* "It's rather late for you."

"This could not wait until morning," he said, brimming with happiness.

"Oh?" The single word was full of dread and hope. Hope that his cousin had finally made a decision about his choice of bride, and dread for who it would be. After what he witnessed earlier, he knew Horatio had asked for Theodora's hand. And it was clear that she had accepted. Bracing himself for the inevitable, he sucked in a deep breath and waited for the final blow that would shatter his entire being.

With a bright smile that seemed to mock Damian, Horatio said, "I have asked Miss Claudia Ashton for her hand in marriage, and she has accepted."

All breath escaped his body and Damian was left speechless. *Horatio had not proposed to Theodora?* Theodora was not engaged to Horatio. His mind was still wrapping itself around the words when his cousin pleaded his case for marrying Miss Ashton.

"I am very fond of her, and she will make an excellent bride. She wants to learn to sail and travel the world with me." Damian was about to argue, was about to state that the whole purpose for his cousin to marry was to prepare him to become the next earl, to take on the responsibility of the earldom, not to neglect his duties. "And I believe there is someone who has caught your eye, and before you argue with me, please just listen," he said with a firmness Damian had not heard from his cousin before.

Damian would listen, but it would not change anything. Despite Horatio's revelation, Theodora still deserved more than what he could offer. Damian kept to the murky depths of darkness, rarely entertained, and was a scarred beast who hadn't been able to save his family from fire, a broken heart from loved ones lost, or from his own fear and insecurities.

"You're wrong." Horatio's statement disrupted his rambling thoughts.

"I'm wrong?"

"Yes. I know what you're thinking. It has been consuming you. You have locked yourself away believing you don't deserve love and happiness." His cousin's gaze bore into him. "Aunt Esther and I have discussed this at length, so there is no use arguing against it."

What was it with his aunt and cousin that they felt constantly determined to intervene in his life? "And you're both—"

"No matter how hard you try, you'll never push us away. We care about you. We love you, Damian. Theresa loves you, too.

She misses you. You should write to her, put the past to rest. And Miss Theodora . . ." Horatio's words trailed away with that final name.

Theodora.

Damian didn't know what to say, how to respond. Much like when Theodora had confessed her feelings for him. The wall he'd built around his heart was crumbling, and it terrified him. Dreams he hadn't dared to dream for more than a decade started to rise from the depths of his soul, demanding he take notice.

He turned away, unable to look at his cousin. So much doubt and sadness weighed him down. Was he strong enough to let go of the past?

A gentle hand cupped his shoulder. "You love her. Do not let the past dictate your future."

"I don't know—"

Horatio shook his head, halting Damian's words. "Because you haven't tried. All these years, you believed your only course was to relinquish the earldom and hide away in some dark corner, but you're wrong. Face your demons, face *your* face, once and for all, and then let go of the past and embrace the present, for you never know what the future holds."

Such wise words from someone so young.

The two of them talked—well, Horatio did most of the talking—and by the time his cousin left, Damian was questioning his entire existence. His entire reason for keeping to the shadows.

Trying to relieve the pain his head, he pressed his fingers to his temples. One touched warm flesh, the other hard, unfeeling leather. A deep sigh rankled through his body. With slow, deliberate steps, Damian moved toward the window, catching his reflection against the inky night sky.

You can do this. You have to do this.

Seconds drew out as he gathered the courage to lift the mask away. Closing his eyes, he removed the cover that had become a protective skin. Coolness caressed his cheek, but he still did not open his eyes. He didn't know how long he stood there, eyes shut tight, as his determination to look upon himself wavered.

You can do this. You have to do this.

Damian slowly opened his eyes. He could not focus on his own reflection, but let his mind drift to the past, before the tragedy, to the loving family that had once been the center of his life. He'd forgotten all the happiness and laughter they'd shared. Hot tears stung the corner of his eyes, not for the loss, but for the years he'd wasted.

Only once he slipped the mask back onto his face did he look at his reflection. But this time he did not see a scarred beast. He saw a man with possibilities on the horizon.

And with the rising sun also came clarity. He knew, without a doubt, what he wanted. He also knew that his cousin was right. He had put the past to rest. It was now time to join the living.

With his mind set, he began to plan for the evening.

TONIGHT WAS THE last night at Grimsby Hall. Anxiety and heartache had been consuming Theodora all day. Would she see Damian before they departed or would he conceal himself, a mere silhouette, watching in the darkness?

"It's time to go down for dinner," Aunt Imogene said in a gentle tone as she entered Theodora's room.

"Why won't he talk to me, Aunt Imogene?" The words brushed past her lips.

She sucked in a deep breath and then on a long, slow exhale, said, "I don't know, my girl. What I do know is that you love him, and I believe he cares for you. Perhaps once Mr. Eastwick's engagement to Miss Ashton is announced, he will be able to feel more at ease." She embraced Theodora. "Let's enjoy this last night. Things will look brighter tomorrow."

Evelina joined them and then they walked to the drawing room together. Once all the guests had arrived, they paraded toward the dining hall. There was a certain melancholy in the air, as if everyone was a little sad to see the house party coming to a close. There had been no gossip or dramatics over the past two weeks, just amiable companionship. Even news of Miss Raine's elopement had not come as a surprise to those present—well, except to Mrs. Raine, who'd left in a panic to inform Lord Raine.

As everyone took their places at the table, Theodora glanced up toward the small balcony. She suspected he was not there. Was he still even in residence? Her heart thudded as tears threatened her resolve. There would be time soon enough to indulge in her tears. She blinked them away and shifted her focus to those around her when she noticed that no one was standing at the place at the bottom of the table. A moment later she discovered why.

A calm hush ascended over the room as Damian, the Earl of Grimsby took his place at the bottom of the table. He still wore the half-mask, but his features and stance seemed lighter, as if a weight had been lifted from his shoulders. He greeted Lady Dufferin and Lady Vernon, who were sitting to his right and left.

As per usual, the food smelled delicious, the conversation was pleasant, but Theodora hardly noticed any of what was occurring around her, too caught up over the sight of Damian sitting with his guests, partaking in a meal. And when dinner concluded, the men did not loiter behind, but went to the drawing room with the ladies.

Theodora had wanted to approach Damian, but she was unsure what his presence meant. They hadn't even made eye contact. A glimmer of hope edged its way through the sadness she'd been experiencing just a short time ago.

"What do you think he's about this evening?" she asked her sister under her breath.

Evelina's gaze focused on Damian as he went to the piano. "Perhaps he's trying to show you that he is putting the past to rest."

A moment later, he began to play a beautiful sonata. She

closed her eyes as the notes and chords filled her soul, giving rise to hope. Images of a waltz under a moonlit sky swirled through her mind. The memory of a passionate kiss infiltrated her senses.

Applause brought her back into the moment. She opened her eyes to find numerous guests surrounding the piano, praising Damian for his playing.

Theodora felt almost overwhelmed by the emotions coursing through her. She wanted to go to him, to have a moment alone with him. She'd never had to share his music with anyone before, and she found it rather unsettling. She continued to watch as guests encircled him, keeping her from him.

Her heart pounded with firm thumps, and as her fingers went to soothe the ache in her chest, they came in contact with the cameo her mother had given her.

Never be afraid of desire. Her dearest mama's words echoed in her mind.

Theodora was not afraid, but what if the man in question was?

There were too many distractions and emotions. She required solitude, to think and let her heart speak. She whispered to her sister, "I'm going to retire. I'm feeling out of sorts."

Evelina responded in kind, "I think a certain music room would provide the quiet you require. I'll let Aunt Imogene know."

"Thank you," she mouthed, then snuck away.

THE ACCOLADES FOR his music were almost overwhelming, and yet the one person he hoped would take notice had just left the room. Could she no longer stand the sight of him?

As Lady Danielle took her place at the harp, preparing to entertain the guests, Damian snuck away, free to wallow in his mistakes. As he trudged toward his music room, the sweet sounds of the piano drifted toward him.

Was he only imagining the sound just as he thought he had the other night? He picked up his pace, and as he reached the closed door, he knew the music was real. He put his hand on the door and felt the chords vibrate through the wood. This was the deciding moment, the moment he both desired and dreaded. But he was past the point of retreat.

The music rushed his senses as he opened the door. And there, sitting at the piano, was his heart's desire, the woman he loved with all his heart, with all his soul.

He didn't know if he could say all the words he wanted to, not yet at least, but he hoped and prayed it would be enough. The moment the music stopped, he went to her and said the words he'd wanted to say for so long.

"I need you." He cupped her face in his hand and held it gently. He still didn't understand why she wanted to be part of his life, why she didn't run away in fear, but he was thankful Theodora had been sent to him. He looked into her lovely blue eyes, full of hope and renewal. "I need you." The whispered words quavered from his lips.

"I'm right here." She stood, then raised up on tiptoes and started to remove his mask. She'd removed it once before, and just as before, it was incredibly intimate. But this time he did not feel vulnerable. Her fingers brushed across the scar. "And I always will be, loving you, just as I do now," she said as she trailed kisses along his cheek to his mouth.

Damian melted into her kiss. It was a kiss for his wounded and tormented soul to melt into. To kiss her forever would never be long enough.

He didn't know it until she'd spoken the words, but they were the ones he had longed to hear his entire life. "I love you, Theodora."

"I think I loved you from the moment I saw you," she whispered between kisses.

Her confession took him aback. He'd felt an instant attraction to her, too, but hadn't believed that it could be real. "Why? How?"

"Your eyes." She cupped his scarred cheek and stroked it with a gentle finger. "Your eyes are filled with goodness." She tilted her head, staring intently into his eyes. "There was sadness and pain, but the goodness shone through, and I knew . . ."

Her words trailed as tears filled her eyes. Were they tears of uncertainty? The pounding in his heart was threatening his resolve, causing doubt to ripple through the moment. He had to know . . . was she having second thoughts? "Theodora?"

She shook her head as she smiled, then began on a whisper, "I knew that you were the only man for me."

Theodora never ceased to amaze him with her passionate words and incredible faith. He knew of no other way to show her how he felt as he took her mouth in a passionate kiss. Many moments passed before he slowly pulled back. There was one more confession he must speak.

"Do you remember when you asked what my inspiration was?"

"Yes."

"Love. The desire and need to be loved. To have someone who knew me, my mind, my thoughts, my soul . . . intimately." He brushed kisses across her lips as he confessed, "You are my inspiration."

"You are mine," she said, her words full of the love flowing between them.

And once again, he lowered his lips and took her mouth in a gentle kiss, one that his tired and wounded heart relished. He didn't know what the future held or why this vibrant and beautiful woman loved him, but he would spend the rest of his life cherishing this most precious gift.

"Theodora," he whispered as he nibbled her lips. "Marry me."

She pulled back and looked into his eyes. "I thought you would never ask," she said with a wide smile.

Epilogue

DAMIAN WAS ENJOYING a peaceful afternoon in the comfort of his study. Never in his wildest dreams would he have imagined being this blissfully happy with another person. Theodora had taught him so much about life and love, but most importantly, she helped him put the past to rest. Because of her unconditional love, Damian had, once and for all, removed the mask he'd been hiding behind and faced the world. Much to his surprise, people did not fear him or the scars. Years of worry, regret, and blame slowly dissipated as he accepted that his father and brother's deaths were not his fault. He wished he had done things differently with his sister all those years ago, but both his aunt's and cousin's encouragement prompted him to write Theresa. Much to his delight and surprise, she was enthusiastic to return to England with her husband and children for a visit.

Damian knew he could not change anything that had already happened, but he could live in the present, and enjoy the blessings afforded to him and his family. His cousin was happily married to Miss Ashton, and Aunt Esther was enjoying a blossoming friendship with Theodora.

Damian leaned back in his chair, admiring the rays of pinks and oranges that streaked across the sky that reminded him of—

"It's time!" He heard his wife's cry echo through the house, startling both him and Shadow.

He jumped up and rushed from his study, colliding with Howard in the corridor. "Pardon me, Lord—"

"Damian! Come quickly!" Theodora's cry echoed once again.

"She's in her private parlor." The words rushed from the Howard's mouth just as Shadow rushed toward them with panicked excitement.

"It's all right," Damian said as he petted the large dog's head. Clearly the dog knew that something was happening.

"Don't worry, my lord, Shadow will be well watched over, and the household staff is ready to assist in whatever way. Go to Lady Grimsby."

He supposed the words were meant to be reassuring, but this was not a house party where things could be planned and executed with precision.

Damian rushed to his wife's private parlor. Several young servants were congregated outside the room, and the moment they saw him, they moved aside, allowing him to pass. The door was slightly ajar, and he could hear Theodora's soothing words drift across the room.

"It's all right, sweet girl," she cooed. "Shh, it's all right."

A sense of love, awe, and admiration washed over him at the sight of his wife as he entered the room, comforting Luna. She was gently stroking the top of her head while offering calming words.

"May I come in?" he asked in a hushed tone.

Aunt Esther looked over to him. "Come in," she whispered. "I will go see how Shadow is doing."

Damian approached his wife, who was sitting next to a large wooden crate, with caution so as not to startle the dog. Luna was laying down, her breathing heavy but not alarmingly so.

"It shouldn't be long now," Theodora said, then turned her attention back on the dog, who adjusted her position and was now raising her tail. She seemed to strain for a short time before something began to emerge. "It's a tail!"

"Is that normal?" Damian had never been around a dog about to birth a litter of puppies. He didn't know if he should be doing anything—though what, he couldn't say.

"Perfectly," she said over her shoulder, her loving eyes meeting his.

Luna appeared calm, like this was the most natural thing in the world. He supposed it was. He watched in awe as she instinctively knew what to do as her first puppy was born. Luna took her time, cleaning her firstborn. A short time later, she appeared to strain again, and before too long, another puppy was delivered.

Hours passed, candles were lit, the fireplace was stoked, and all Luna's puppies were born. It was a wonderous sight watching her tend to her young, who were all now curled about her warm belly, squeaking and suckling to their hearts' content.

Damian sat on the floor behind Theodora, then rubbed her shoulders. "You must be tired, my dear."

"Nothing compared to Luna. She did beautifully." His loving wife leaned back, resting against him. He loved the feel of her body against him.

He kissed the top of her head, enjoying the moment. "That she did."

"How is Shadow?" Concern laced her words.

"He was very anxious and unsure. I think he misses her."

Theodora glanced up at him. "That's understandable. They've been inseparable since I snuck her into the house."

They watched as the puppies curled into their mother, drifting off to sleep, content. With each passing day, Damian felt that contentment more and more. The past would always be part of who he was, but he was no longer letting it dictate his actions or drown his thoughts in misery.

Damian leaned in and brushed a gentle kiss across her lips. "Thank you," he sighed as he leaned his forehead against hers.

The spot between her brows her brows crinkled. "For what?"

He spoke without worry or hesitation the words his heart

longed to say. "For being my moon, for lighting the darkest part of my soul."

Theodora cupped his cheek, just like she'd done so many times before, and just like before, Damian cherished the love she offered. "You are my world, my passion and desire. You are my everything."

With this confession, Theodora offered him a beautifully endearing smile. Damian had truly found his soulmate.

About the Author

Bestselling, award-winning author, Alanna Lucas pens Regency-set historicals filled with romance, adventure, and of course, happily ever afters. When she is not daydreaming of her next travel destination, Alanna can be found researching, spending time with family, tending to her garden, or going for long walks. She makes her home in California with her husband and children, and too many books to count.

Just for the record, you can never have too many handbags or books. And travel is a must.